GLASS CLOSET

The Price of Silence, The Triumph of Voice

IAM OBSYDIAN

Copyright © 2023 by Iam Obsydian

All rights reserved.

No part of this publication may be reproduced, distributed, or transmitted in any form or by any means, including photocopying, recording, or other electronic or mechanical methods, without the prior written permission of the author, except for the use of brief quotations in a book review.

This is a work of fiction. Names, characters, places, and incidents either are the product of the author's imagination or are used fictitiously, and any resemblance to actual persons, living or dead, businesses, companies, events, or locales is entirely coincidental.

To the silenced and the sung. To the hidden and the proud. To those journeying towards truth, and those seeking understanding. This is your story, too.

Step in, brave reader. Together, let's dare to change the world, one page at a time.

<3

❧ 1 ❧
QUIET CORNERS

I'm Ethan, a seventeen-year-old living in my own pocket of silence within the deafening orchestra of life. My room, cast in the warm glow from the lamp on my desk, is my sanctuary. It's the one place where serenity washes over me, where I am unequivocally myself. Here, there are no judgments, no expectations, only me, and my faithful companions: my books.

The walls of my room serve as a chronicle of my journey. Adorned with posters of esteemed authors and cherished books, punctuated with poignant literary quotes, they provide an insight into the world of a boy who finds solace in fictional realms. A boy who often prefers the companionship of characters over real people. This room, with its soothing familiarity and reassuring security, is a tranquil haven.

My room is compact but inviting. Shelves, sagging slightly under the weight of books from every genre, are a testament to my love for literature. Each book offers an escape, a portal into a myriad of different worlds and lives. They've been my faithful confidants during countless sleepless nights, their narratives acting as lullabies, their characters providing companionship amidst my solitude.

Tonight, ensconced in my favourite reading nook by the window, the soft blanket providing warmth against the chill of the night, I'm lost in a world of fantasy. I relish the idea of shrugging off reality and diving headfirst into realms where I can be a knight, a magician, a hero who battles dragons and rescues entire kingdoms. Tonight, however, I'm not a hero. I'm just a young boy seeking solace in stories.

The hushed hum of the night outside punctuates my reading, providing a soothing soundtrack. As I delve deeper into the book, the characters seem to materialise in the quiet of my room, their voices whispering their tales in the silence.

This immersion allows me to experience the adventure, the romance, and the heartbreaks of these characters, to vicariously feel their joy, their despair, their victories. It's a temporary reprieve, a much-needed liberation from my problems, worries, and insecurities.

Within the universe of books, there's no need for pretence or a facade. There's no need to fit into a predefined mould or concern myself with societal judgments. Here, in this quiet sanctuary, I can just be Ethan.

People often tell me I need to "get out more," to "make more friends." They fail to understand that this world of words and silence is my reality. I've found friendship within the characters that populate my books, discovered wisdom nestled within the lines, and found a comforting silence that speaks volumes.

I won't deny the occasional pangs of loneliness that sometimes accompany my solitude, or the yearning for a connection that extends beyond the confines of the printed pages. However, for now, I find contentment within this peaceful isolation, in this quiet corner of the universe that I've claimed as my own.

Tonight, as I turn the pages of my book, I'm a young bibliophile secure in his sanctuary. Outside, the world continues its cacophonous symphony—laughter and chatter, the buzz of cars, and the blaring music. But here, ensconced in my quiet corner, I am at peace. Here, I am home.

※

THE SOFT HUES OF DAWN PAINT A NEW DAY ON THE CANVAS outside my window. With a reluctant sigh, I put away my recent sanctuary, a captivating tale of enchantments and mythical creatures. The magic of its pages is replaced with a reality less fantastical and more daunting: high school.

Every day here is another round in the arena of adolescent social politics, where I'm a misfit in a place that should feel familiar. As I step into the high school's buzzing corridors, a wave of chatter washes over me, echoing the bewildering rhythm of a dance I cannot seem to grasp. The jovial clusters of students, each absorbed in their world, remind me that I am an observer here, not a participant.

Navigating through the labyrinthine crowd, I keep my gaze lowered, focusing on the path ahead. The school's walls, enlivened by posters of upcoming events, form a jarring contrast with the literary posters that adorn my room. The dichotomy between these fantasy worlds and the stark reality stirs a yearning within me for the comforting haven of my books.

Within the classroom, my peers congregate around tables, engaged in vivacious discussions about weekend plans, their jargon foreign and elusive. Football games, parties, dates — all universes I don't belong to.

I gravitate towards my usual spot, a solitary island at the back of the room. From here, I spectate the theatrics of teenage life unfolding before me.

My peers jest and guffaw with an air of carefreeness, a stark contrast to the heavy silence that cloaks me. An intriguing question crosses my mind: what is it like to be part of their world? To belong, to effortlessly blend into the social fabric, to not feel like a stranger in your own life?

But then, I find solace in remembering the narratives I've been lost in, the adventures I've lived through the characters who were different, misunderstood, outsiders. These characters taught me that there's an inherent beauty in being unique, in not conforming to the mould. It's these characters whose resonating words of wisdom give me the fortitude to survive another day on this battlefield of adolescence.

Lunchtime hits the hardest. It's when the gnawing loneliness becomes palpable, when the silence is deafening. The cafeteria, a tumultuous sea of animated conversation, presents a navigational challenge. My refuge in this storm is the library, a sanctuary amidst the chaos. Amongst the rows of books, I find a fragment of the peace that my home offers.

And so, my day unfolds as a series of discomfort, solitude, and fleeting moments of tranquility. Each moment serves as a constant reminder of my place—or rather, my lack thereof—in this world. But with every step I take, every awkward moment I endure, I am bolstered by the strength of the characters I've come to admire. Their stories serve as my shield, their struggles a source of inspiration.

As the final bell tolls, signalling the end of another challenging day, I collect my things, washed over by a tide of relief. I've survived another day in the arena. My heart beats in anticipation for the sanctuary of my room, my books, my quiet corner.

In this world, I may be the introvert, the outsider, the bookworm. But I know that I am also the knight, the sorcerer, the hero of my narrative. This realisation gives me the strength to face another day because, in the end, aren't we all characters in the grand tapestry of our own lives, searching for our place in this cosmic narrative we call life?

As I exit the school building, the late afternoon sun stretches out long shadows across the concrete in its final encore before nightfall. My heart aches for the familiar comfort of home, the solace found within the pages of my books. Yet, there's a specific twinge, a knot that forms within my chest, one that's become a familiar guest. A knot that tightens every time I see him - Lorence.

Lorence, with his disarmingly charming grin and warm hazel eyes. Lorence, who thrives within a bubble of constant companionship, his laughter acting as a beacon in the everyday chaos of our school. Lorence, who possesses an uncanny ability to stir my heart into a frantic race and paint a vivid blush across my cheeks.

There he is on the football field, his figure a silhouette against the setting sun, drawing my gaze like a moth helplessly captivated by a flame. I watch as he sends the football sailing through the air, his laughter reaching even me, stationed in my solitary vantage point.

But with each heartbeat, each stolen glance, a wave of confusion and fear sweeps over me. I try to dismiss these feelings as mere admiration, convincing myself that I desire to emulate him – to be more outgoing, more popular, more... normal. Yet, I am painfully aware that this is not the complete truth.

Underneath the surface, there's a deeper connection, an unspoken longing. A yearning to know him, to be near him, that goes beyond the confines of simple friendship. It's an emotion I struggle to comprehend, a feeling that instills fear within me.

As my stomach churns amidst the turmoil of my emotions, my mind buzzes with questions that I am too frightened to confront. Why do I feel this way? What does it signify? I am definitely...

I quickly squash the emerging thought. I can't possibly be...that. It's deemed wrong, isn't it? Society says so, my classmates jest about it, and the church I was brought up in preaches fervently against it.

A sharp pang of guilt cuts through me, fear gripping the edges of my consciousness. My secret, my concealed struggle, feels like an insurmountable burden. Thus, I resort to my tried-and-true escape – I retreat into the sanctuary of my mind, the refuge offered by my imagination, the comforting solace of my books.

Forcing my gaze away from Lorence, I attempt to ignore the quickening of my pulse, the stirring within my stomach. I remind myself that this is treacherous terrain, a path better left away.

At home, in my quiet corner, I immerse myself within the pages of another novel. Tonight, it's a tale of love between a prince and a commoner girl. As I absorb their stolen glances, the flutters of their hearts, their secret kisses, my thoughts inevitably wander towards Lorence.

But I promptly bury the thought, pushing it into the deepest recesses of my mind. I can't afford to entertain such desires, such whimsical fancies. I tell myself it's nothing more than a fleeting fantasy, a narrative that will never bear the fruit of reality.

As night descends, a blanket of darkness envelops the world outside my window. The only sounds that permeate the silence are the steady ticking of the clock and the soft rustle of turning pages. Yet within me, a storm is brewing – a tempest of confusion, fear, and suppressed desires.

Thus, this is my plight, my clandestine turmoil. Each day, I present the world with a smile, concealing my struggle behind a mask of normalcy. Behind this mask, behind the seemingly content smiles, I'm a boy grappling with his feelings, struggling to comprehend his place in the grand tapestry of the world.

Each night, I pray for clarity, understanding, and acceptance. I yearn for the day when I can gaze at Lorence devoid of fear, guilt, or confusion. But for now, I must persevere. For now, I must maintain my façade. For now, my secret remains guarded, my quiet corner preserved, my sanctuary safe.

And so, I turn another page, immersing myself in another narrative. Within these stories, I find a measure of peace, an escape, a sense of understanding. Above all, they offer me hope - hope for a day when I can fully be me.

For the time being, this is all I possess. This is all I can clutch onto.

With a heavy heart, a tumultuous mind, and a spirit clinging to hope, I continue on my journey. A journey that's distinctly mine.

※

LIFE AT HIGH SCHOOL IS A BATTLEFIELD, A CONSTANT TUG of war between belonging and alienation. I have always been a bystander, a silent observer in the face of this war. But, there are times when silence feels like a burden too heavy to bear. One such instance occurs on a seemingly ordinary day, marked only by the incident that unfolds in the schoolyard.

During lunch, while making my usual beeline to the library, I come across a crowd gathering in the far corner of the schoolyard. There's an odd sense of anticipation in the air, an ugly excitement that makes my skin crawl. As I draw closer, the scene becomes all too clear. A small group of jocks are huddled around someone, their laughter echoing in the chilling silence.

The kid at the centre is Miles, a quiet boy who, like me, is more comfortable in the background than the limelight. The jocks are jeering, their words laced with venom. The crowd watches in silent amusement, their inaction louder than any words. A knot of dread twists in my gut, a lump forming in my throat. It's a scene all too familiar, a scene that feeds my worst fears.

My mind becomes a whirlwind of thoughts. Fear, outrage, anxiety, all intertwined. The laughter echoes in my ears, amplifying the feeling of dread. I want to help, to intervene, but fear holds me back. Fear of drawing attention, fear of becoming a target, fear of revealing my own secret.

This is the reality of our school, a place where different is deemed wrong. Miles is being bullied for his nerdiness, and I can't help but think: what if they find out about me? What if they find out about my secret? The thought fills me with a bone-chilling fear, freezing me on the spot.

It's a silent reminder of the hostility that lies under the facade of normalcy. The unspoken rules of high school: conform or be ridiculed. The message is clear and fear-inducing. Keep your head down, fit in, don't be different. And for someone like me, someone harbouring a secret that's deemed 'different', this message is a nightmare.

I feel a tug on my heart as I look at Miles, his face red and eyes filled with unshed tears. My heart aches for him, for his humiliation, for his pain. I wish I had the courage to help, to stand against the wrong, but all I have is fear and self-preservation.

I retreat, my heart pounding, my palms sweaty. I take one last look at the scene, a reminder of my deepest fears, and then walk away. As I distance myself from the sight, the laughter and jeering grow faint, but the impact is lasting.

I retreat to the comfort of the library, to the solitude of my books. I lose myself in tales of heroes and bravery, wishing for a fraction of their courage. I wish for a world where Miles doesn't have to face humiliation for being different, a world where I don't have to live in fear of my secret being discovered.

But wishes, they're just that—wishes. Reality is a different story.

They're the daydreams that float around in our heads, making us smile on bad days and giving us something to aim for. They're the superheroes of our own stories, always arriving just in time to save the day in our imaginations. We paint them in the brightest colours and frame them in the ideal scenarios, believing for a moment that they're within our reach.

But, wishes aren't reality. They don't have a physical address or an expiry date. They're like the clouds, always there, always changing, but you can never really touch them. Wishes are the 'what if' and the 'if only', the things we hold onto when reality is a little too real.

Reality, though, is a whole different game. It's the stuff that actually happens, not just the things we wish would happen. Reality is the test we forgot to study for, the alarm that goes off too early in the morning, the bullying in the schoolyard. It doesn't care about our daydreams or our ideal scenarios. It just is.

Sometimes, it feels like wishes and reality are on different teams, playing different sports on different fields. But that doesn't mean we should stop wishing. We just need to remember that wishes are the starting line, not the finish line. They give us something to aim for, something to work towards. They're the vision, but reality—that's where the action happens.

So, I hold onto my wishes, not as some magical solution that will make everything better, but as a compass to guide me. Because I know that wishes can't change the world on their own. I've got to do that part myself. But hey, having a direction to go in? That's half the battle right there.

Life has a way of moving on, of pushing us forward, and so I move forward. With fear in my heart and hope in my soul, I brace myself for another day. Another day of secrets, another day of fear, another day of wishes and of quiet corners.

Because even in the face of fear, life goes on. And so do I.

※

THERE'S A SOOTHING TRANQUILITY FOUND IN THE stillness of the night. As the world outside succumbs to a profound slumber, the familiar confines of my room seem to pulse with a life of their own, shadows murmuring stories of solitude and refuge. Surrounded by the comforting scent of weathered books and dog-eared pages, I lose myself in the labyrinth of my thoughts, wading through the turbulent waters of my intensifying fears.

In the muted serenity of my room, my own heartbeat is the loudest sound, each pulsation a reflection of the relentless questions that whirl in my mind. Queries about my identity, my clandestine secret, the bewildering rush of emotions threatening to shatter the fragile facade of normalcy I painstakingly maintain each day.

My thoughts stray to Lorence, his image stirring an unfamiliar flutter in my chest. I grapple to comprehend the surge of emotions that engulfs me every time he crosses my mind, every shared glance. It's an inexplicable magnetism, an attraction that unnerves me. Yet, beneath the fear, there's a peculiar warmth, an intriguing familiarity that stirs deep within.

Fear and desire, two contradictory forces wage war within me. The dread of being alien, of facing judgment, of ostracisation, is a formidable adversary. Yet, the desire for acceptance, understanding, and the freedom to love without restraint matches it in strength. It's an internal war, with both sides vying for victory.

Staring into the velvety blackness of the night, my mind spirals into a whirl of possibilities. What would life be if I could just be myself? If I could express my feelings for Lorence without the spectre of fear looming ominously over me? The idea fills me with profound longing, a yearning for a life emancipated from fear, unshackled from societal expectations.

But reality is a ruthless anchor. I exist in a world that is too often unkind to those who dare to be different. The bullying incident involving Miles serves as a chilling reminder of the cost of divergence. The laughter, the mockery, the humiliation – they resonate within me, fuelling my darkest fears. The thought of enduring such contempt, such malice, is unbearable. I can't bear to surrender my quiet corner, my sanctuary, my refuge.

As the night deepens, the burden of my secret grows heavier. It's a secret that resides within me, a secret that is a part of my essence. I'm gay. The words feel strange, even within my own mind, yet they resonate with an irrefutable truth. A truth I'm terrified to acknowledge, terrified to unveil.

Yet, under the protective shroud of night, the truth doesn't seem as fearsome. It feels integral to me, an essential piece of the complex mosaic that is Ethan. It doesn't confine me, but it contributes to my identity.

Tears sting my eyes, a wave of relief and fear washing over me. Acceptance is a double-edged sword, offering solace yet stirring a tempest of anxiety. But for now, I bask in the solitary moment, the quiet acknowledgment, the fleeting sense of peace.

As sleep begins to weave its enchanting spell, I yield to its soothing lull. Sailing into the realm of dreams, I clutch onto a glimmer of hope, a beacon in the tumultuous storm of my fears. Hope for understanding, hope for acceptance, hope for a day when I can be myself without trepidation.

In the secluded corner of my room, in the secret recesses of my heart, I make a silent vow. A pledge to the scared, lost boy inside, that someday, he'll find his path. Someday, he'll step out of the shadows, accept his truth, and stride forth with unwavering confidence.

With that, I surrender to the encroaching night, letting my dreams carry me away into a world painted with hope, acceptance, and love. The night might be dark and fraught with fears, but it's also the canvas of dreams, dreams that holds the promise of a new dawn, a fresh start.

Drifting into a restless sleep, a single phrase reverberates in the secret corners of my mind - I am gay, and it's okay. I am gay, and it's okay. I am gay, and it's okay.

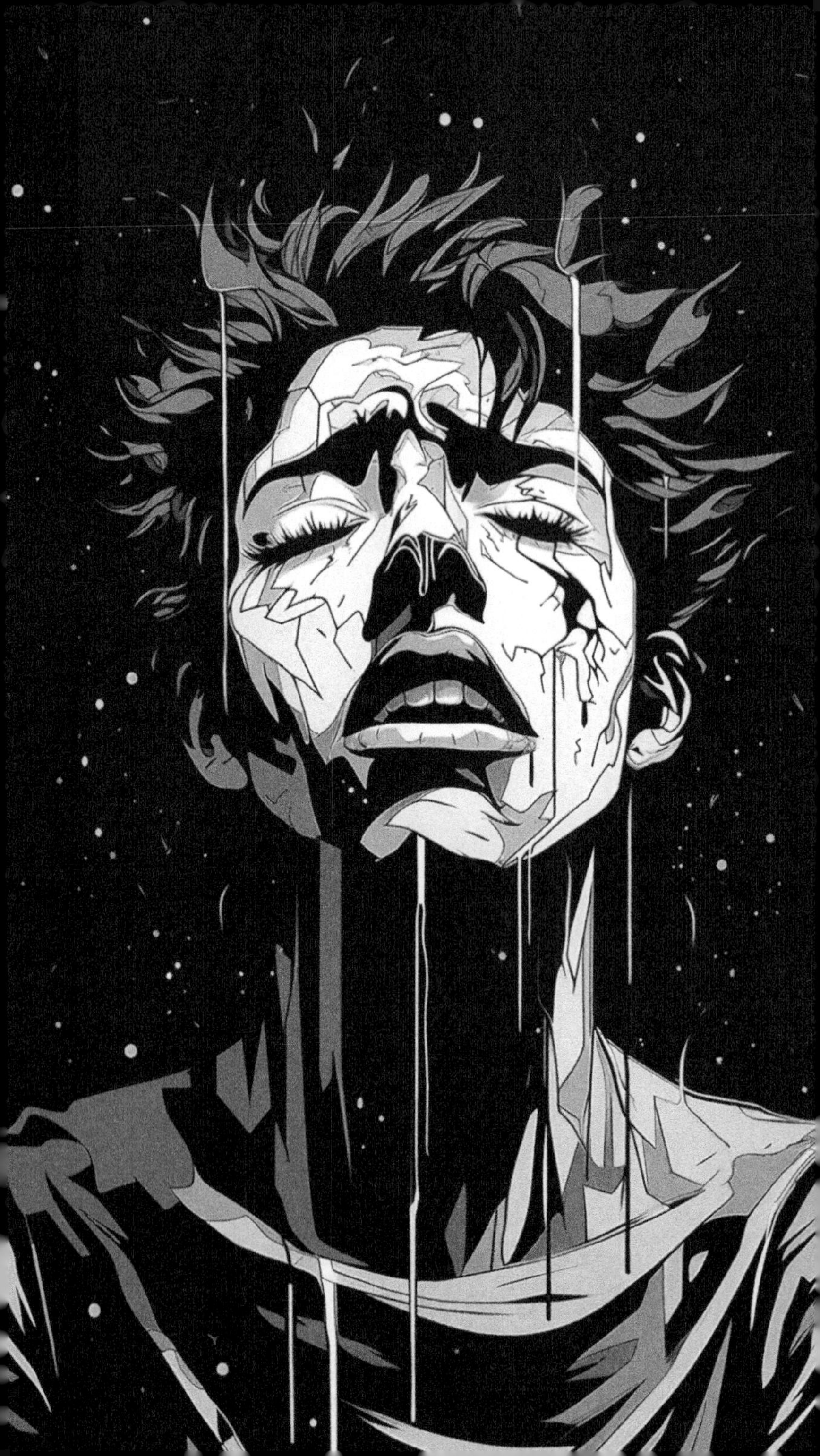

❧ 2 ❦
UNMASKING SHADOWS

I've always understood the unnerving potency of silence. This afternoon, as school empties out, I come to appreciate its menace in a harsh new light.

The late afternoon sun slants into a secluded corner I like around the school grounds, casting elongated shadows that seem to pulsate with a disturbing rhythm. My heart thrashes wildly in my chest, each beat echoing the terror that surges through my veins. The insidious whispers that have trailed me lead me here, away from the relative safety of bustling classrooms and watchful eyes.

Jackson, Mark, and Bryan form a foreboding trio in front of me, smiles on their faces that don't quite reach their eyes. The threat hangs heavy in the air, unspoken but unmistakably clear. Rumours, the insidious beast, have burrowed into every nook and cranny, eventually exposing my secret.

Jackson, the leader, crosses his arms over his chest, his brows furrowed in a menacing glare directed at me. His voice, when he speaks, is deceptively soft, the sound slicing through the unsettling silence. "Heard a little rumour about you, Ethan."

The silence that follows his words reverberates, deafening and absolute.

My mind races, searching for an escape, for some way to evade this impending threat. But the icy glint in Jackson's eyes tells me there's no escaping this confrontation. He's waiting. Waiting for a denial, waiting for an admission, waiting for a crack in my defences.

Something about my quiet life, my solitude, seems to paint a target on my back. An acceptable casualty in their ruthless game. Yet, the fear and trembling uncertainty don't solely stem from their looming threat. They arise from the half-truths and the burgeoning acceptance stirring within me.

The rumour revolves around my sexual orientation. Rumours about the way I walk, how I behave, how I look at Lorence when he walks past me.

Is it so wrong? Is it a sin to harbour these feelings? The world's echoed disapproval resonates with lessons ingrained in me over the years. Yet, the truth I am beginning to embrace whispers a different tune. It's okay, Ethan. It's okay to be you.

"Something to say in your defence, bookworm?" Mark, usually the more subdued one, interjects, his words slicing through my spiralling thoughts. His tone conveys boredom, as if my fear and predicament are mundane, commonplace.

"No," I respond, my voice barely a whisper, strangled by the throes of fear and uncertainty. They're expecting a denial, expecting me to dismiss the rumour with a derisive laugh. But the words remain unspoken, lodged within my newfound honesty and acceptance.

I'm not ready to scream my truth from the rooftops. Still, the shroud of denial feels suffocating, intolerable. Perhaps my silence, my refusal to dismiss the truth, serves as my initial act of defiance, the first stepping stone on the path to self-acceptance.

A cruel smile inches across Bryan's face, his eyes glittering with a dark promise of pain. "Well, then. Seems like we have some business to discuss."

As the sun dips below the horizon, shadows creep and lengthen, almost symbolic of the impending darkness threatening to engulf me. A voice in the back of my mind trembles at the thought of what's to come. Yet another voice, softer but more resolute, whispers words of strength, endurance, and acceptance.

As I brace myself in this secluded corner, the lingering silence bears witness to my fear, my budding courage, and my unuttered truth. My secret stands exposed to rumours, and there's no turning back. Amid the looming threat and the uncertainty that tugs at the edges of this moment, one thing solidifies in my mind - my quiet corner will never be the same again.

The air is heavy with tension, pierced only by my ragged breathing, the frantic drumming of my heart, and the chill of laughter that hangs ominously in the air.

Bryan's cruel smile persists, heralding a storm poised to unleash its fury. My palms sweat and my legs tremble, struggling to keep me upright, as fear wraps around me like a vice. I am cornered, like a rabbit caught in headlights, with nowhere to run or hide.

Suddenly, Jackson steps forward, his face a mirror reflecting the grim reality I'm on the brink of confronting. His eyes are icy and devoid of empathy as he looms over me.

"So you're one of them, huh?" His voice drips with disgust, his words a venomous whisper in the encroaching dusk.

One of them. The phrase hits like a slap, a pointed reminder of society's scorn for people like me, for those I could love. I open my mouth to protest, to deny, but the words perish before they can breathe. The truth is a bitter pill to swallow, but its taste is growing familiar.

Before I can summon a response, a blow lands on my chest, knocking the wind out of me. I gasp and stumble backward, the harsh reality of my situation hitting me with similar force.

Mark and Bryan close in, their grins a stark contrast to the terror coursing through me. Their blows are swift and ruthless, their derogatory words mirroring the physical onslaught.

"Faggot!"

"You're going to hell!"

Their slurs cut through the air like knives, each syllable a punch to my soul. The physical pain is nearly unbearable, but it's the verbal assault, the hate-filled epithets, the explicit homophobia, that stings more.

Bryan, Jackson, and Mark - their names ricochet in my mind with every hit, each slur spat out with loathing and revulsion.

"You're a disgrace, Ethan!" Jackson growls, his punch sending a jolt of pain from my ribs. I gasp, my lungs emptying forcefully.

Bryan sneers, his words slicing the frigid air. "You're a sick pervert! There's no place for your kind here!"

Their words, their contempt, their hostility, feel like a vice tightening around my insides. The hate in their voices echoes, syncopating with the brutal reality of my situation. My mind is a whirlwind of pain, terror, and desperation.

"You don't belong here, Ethan. No one wants you here. You're just a filthy fag!" Mark snarls, punctuating his words with another punch to my abdomen. I crumple onto the cold asphalt, its harsh scrape against my skin.

The insults don't cease, the abhorrent words seeping into

my consciousness, their toxic venom infecting every corner of my mind.

"Filthy queer!"

"Cocksucker!"

"Disgusting!"

"You're unnatural!"

"No one will ever love you, you freak!"

The words hang heavy, as if the very air is tainted by their bigotry. Their verbal onslaught, a brutal counterpart to the physical abuse, is designed to break me, to reduce me to less than human. I'm no longer the book-loving introvert. I'm 'one of them,' a target of their irrational hatred, their prejudice.

The pain is overwhelming, yet amidst the onslaught, a surprising emotion rises within me - anger. Anger at the sheer injustice, at the hatred directed at me merely for being myself. The fear persists, now tinged with a bitter rage.

As my vision blurs and darkness creeps in, I cling to that anger, that sense of injustice. Their laughter and scorn fill the air, but their words, intended to shatter me, are stoking a fire within. A fire fuelled by anger, indignation, and an unwavering sense of self. I might not be able to fight back physically, but I can endure, I can survive. In itself, that is a form of rebellion.

The world starts to spin as the hits keep landing, each punch an exclamation mark to their vicious homophobia. I can taste blood in my mouth, can feel the cold pavement pressing against my back, but the physical pain feels distant.

Faced with such monstrous hatred, I find resolve. With every harsh word, every bone-rattling hit, I clutch tighter to my identity.

The last thing I remember is their laughter ringing around me, a cruel symphony scoring my downfall. Darkness creeps in, swallowing the pain, the fear, the humiliation. As consciousness slips away, the bitter taste of reality lingers.

The world is a brutal battleground for a seventeen-year-old boy coming to terms with his sexuality. I've just taken a devastating hit, but as the darkness claims me, one thought shines like a beacon amidst the chaos.

I am Ethan. I am gay. I am not a mistake, not disgusting, not unnatural, not wrong. I am human. I am valid. And no amount of hatred or bigotry can erase that truth.

I am Ethan. I am gay. And I will not be defeated.

Consciousness ebbs and flows, waves of awareness washing over me as sirens wail piercingly, each shriek a jolt of pain in my beaten body. Voices circle me, their words distant and muffled, punctuating the shuffle of urgent footsteps and rustling fabric.

The second my back makes contact with the frigid, unyielding surface of the ambulance stretcher, a whirlwind of activity engulfs me. Cryptic medical terms are tossed around, latex gloves palpating my bruised skin, their cold touch a jarring yet comforting anchor amidst my sea of pain.

The ambulance slices through the night, city lights smearing into streaks of colours outside the small window. It's a dizzying kaleidoscope of confusion, the world spinning around me, leaving me trapped within my battered body.

The hospital is an explosion of sound and motion. As the paramedics push me through the icy, starkly-lit hallways, doctors and nurses dart past, their faces blurred into masks of urgency and concern. Transferred onto a hospital bed, every jolt, every motion sparks fresh waves of pain.

A young woman, a doctor with glasses and a face etched with stern concentration, takes the reins. She assesses my injuries, her hands steady, professional as she investigates the extent of my harm. Her voice is a calm lullaby amidst the storm, the undertone of simmering fury barely concealed.

"How long?" she demands from a paramedic, her voice cutting through the noise.

"Not sure," he replies, voice heavy. "He was unconscious when we found him."

"Damn it," she hisses under her breath before addressing me, her words as crisp as the hospital sheets beneath me. "Ethan, can you hear me? You're in the hospital. You're safe now."

I yearn to respond, to reassure her of my awareness, yet my body remains uncooperative. My eyelids weigh a ton, my mouth is parched, and the edges of my world begin to blur.

Her voice filters through again, orchestrating the chaos, her command bouncing off the sterile walls. Her words are distant, like an echo in a canyon.

Then comes the pinch in my arm. I catch a glimpse of a nurse plunging a needle into an IV line. Seconds later, a wave of lethargy crashes over me, pulling me under.

"Rest now, Ethan," the doctor murmurs, her words a soothing balm on my frayed nerves. "You're safe now."

Her voice, a soft lullaby amidst the chaos, is the last thing I register before succumbing to darkness.

I find myself alone once again, but not in the haven of my room or the tranquil corner of the school library. I'm isolated in a hospital bed, my body a canvas of black and blue, yet there's an unexpected clarity blossoming amidst the pain.

My journey has just started, and my resolve to fight for myself and others like me, those compelled to lurk in the shadows for the sake of love, solidifies. Despite lying in a hospital bed, fractured and bruised, I'm still here. I'm still breathing. And as long as I draw breath, I will fight.

I awaken in a sea of white – white sheets, white walls, the harsh glare of a white light above. Disorientation grips me for a moment, my mind lost in the maze of thoughts. The heavy scent of antiseptic permeates the air, and the beep of machines punctuates the silence. My body is a dead weight, limbs stiff and unresponsive.

An attempt to sit up detonates a shockwave of pain through my body, stealing my breath. Gasping for air, I collapse back onto the pillow, eyes tightly shut as I ride the wave of agony.

When I pry them open again, a face hovers over me – a doctor with eyes hidden behind glasses and a grim expression. He speaks, but his words are distant, muffled by the relentless throb in my head.

"Easy, Ethan," he soothes. "You're safe now. You've been through a lot."

Safe. The word feels alien. I am far from safe. Unbidden, unwelcome images surge through my mind – the bullies' sneers, their harsh words, the blows that descended upon me. The terror, the crushing fear of dying alone in that alley.

Tears spring to my eyes. I turn my head away, a futile attempt to hide my vulnerability. But the tears fall anyway, trailing down my cheeks, soaking the pillow beneath.

"You're safe now, Ethan," the doctor repeats gently. "You're in the hospital. You're going to be okay."

The words ring hollow. I am indeed in a hospital, surrounded by doctors and nurses dedicated to healing, but okay feels like a distant shore.

My thoughts swirl back to the incident, each detail etched into my memory with painful precision. The kicks and punches, the cold ground, the taste of my blood. The fear. The shame. The loneliness.

A nurse enters then, kindness etched on her face as she adjusts the IV in my arm. I watch her, my thoughts a tempest of fear and confusion.

Why me? Why am I the one enduring this? What have I done to earn such cruelty? I am just a boy. A boy who likes boys. My only crime. My only sin.

But to them, it is enough. Enough to cast me as an outcast, a target, a victim.

As I lay in the sterile hospital room, a profound sense of loss engulfs me. A loss not just for myself but for all those who've walked this painful path. All those tormented, beaten, and bullied simply for being true to themselves. For being gay.

Their pain, fear, and despair weigh heavily on me, a knot in my stomach, a lump in my throat. But as the tears continue to fall, a new emotion surfaces - anger.

I am angry. Furious, even. Not a blind rage, not a destructive fury, but a controlled burn, a fire within me. A resolve.

I won't let this defeat me. I won't let them win. I will rise, stronger and more determined. I will stand up for myself and for all those who couldn't. I will turn my pain into power, my fear into fortitude, my shame into strength.

The hospital room doesn't feel so cold anymore. The beeping of the machines becomes a rhythm, a heartbeat, a testament to my resilience. The doctor's words no longer ring hollow. I am safe. But more importantly, I am alive.

The subtle click of the door and a whisper of movement disrupt my introspection. Turning my head, I find my parents in the doorway, their faces drawn, painted with worry. My mother stands there, hands torturing a tissue, eyes pooling with unshed tears. Beside her, my father, always the sturdy pillar, but now, there's a softness in his gaze that seldom shows itself.

Moving silently as the flight of an owl, they step inside

and draw chairs to my bedside. The room shrinks around us, the air dense and stifling. Their worry is a tangible shroud, a comforting yet oppressive blanket. My mouth opens to speak, but the words jam, choked back by a surge of emotion.

"Ethan," my mother's voice quivers, "Oh, Ethan..."

Her trembling hand reaches out to touch my face. The contact ripples through me, stirring a pang of guilt. Their son, their only child, here, bruised and battered on a hospital bed. I can't bear her heartbreak; my eyes slide shut.

"Mum, I..." I begin, my voice a ghostly whisper. She dismisses it with a shake of her head.

"You don't have to say anything," she soothes, her hand catching a rogue tear tracing a path down my cheek. "You're safe now, that's all that matters."

Safe. That word again. It feels like a cruel, twisted jest.

My father, a man of scant words, reaches out, his hand enveloping mine. His grip is firm, anchoring. He remains silent, yet the squeeze of his hand speaks for him. I am not alone. They stand with me.

But they don't know, they can't possibly grasp the truth of the assault. To them, it's a senseless act of violence, a random incident. They're oblivious to the taunts, the slurs, the icy tendrils of fear that clutched my heart each school day. And I'm not ready to shatter their illusion.

"I'm sorry," I murmur, voice fracturing. "I'm so sorry."

"Why are you apologising?" My mother's brow knits in confusion. "You didn't do anything wrong."

But hadn't I? I'd dared to be different, been too weak to conceal my true self. And it's led me here, into this waking nightmare.

My father's grip tightens. "Ethan," he rumbles, his voice gravelly with emotion. "None of this is your fault. You have nothing to apologise for."

I nod, but the guilt persists, a burdensome stone within me.

Time blurs into a symphony of whispered reassurances, gentle touches, shared silences. They don't prod for details or press me to recount the events. Their presence is a soft underscore to their steadfast love.

When they rise to leave, promising a swift return, I watch them go with gratitude tinged with sorrow. I love them, more than words can convey, but I grieve for them, for the impending storm of pain and confusion.

Despite the outpouring of love and support, I know I can't guard my secret indefinitely. I am different, and soon, they will have to know. The prospect of their acceptance or potential rejection instills a fear that overwhelms the confines of the hospital room.

For now, though, they depart believing they know the full story. They believe they're leaving their son, battered and healing. But they're leaving a stranger, a son they don't truly understand.

And I am left alone, eyes fixed on the sterile white ceiling, my thoughts a whirlwind of fear, anticipation, and a glimmer of hope. Maybe, just maybe, things might improve from here.

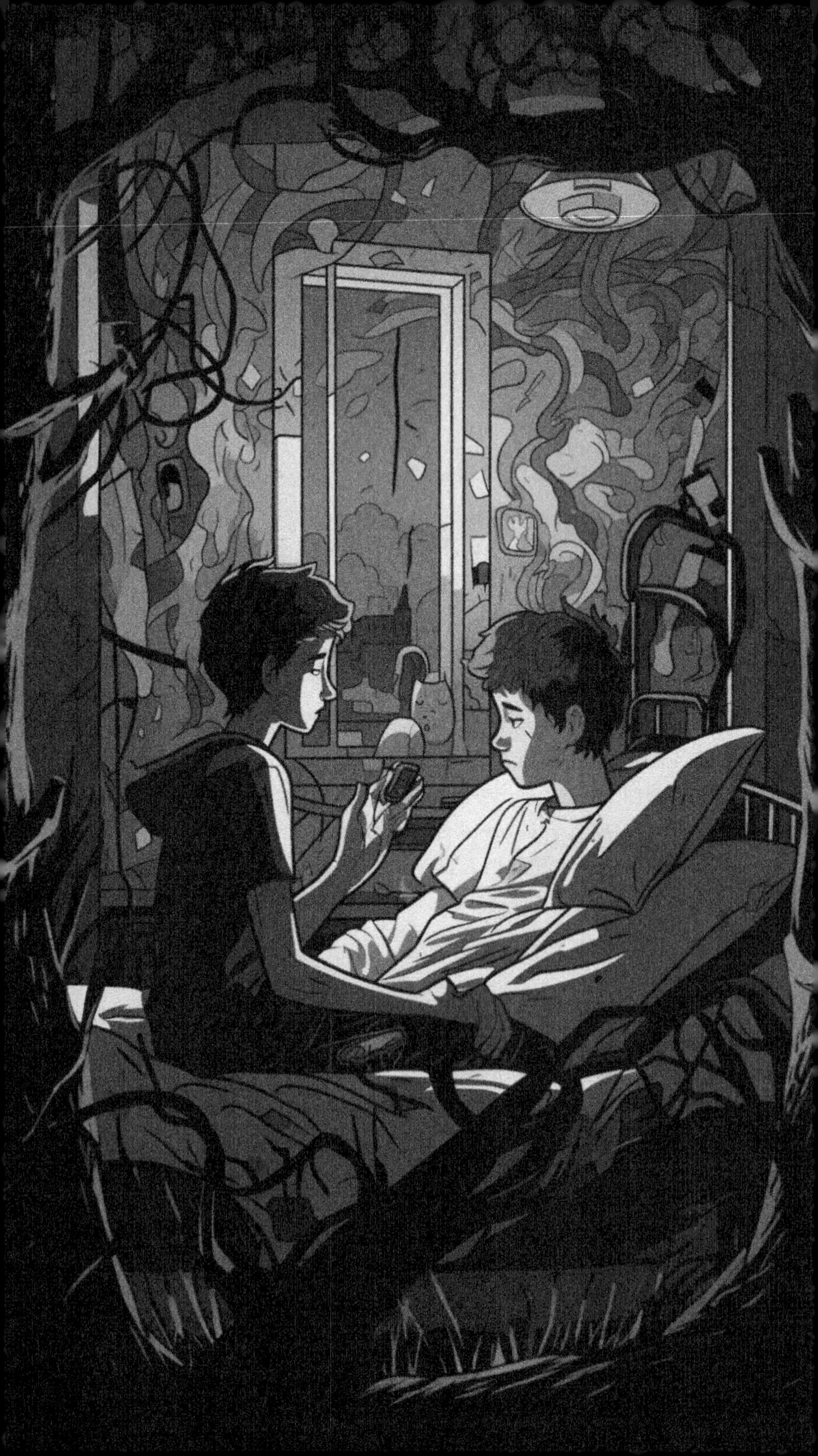

3
THE HOSPITAL HAVEN

Hospital days stretch and condense in strange ways, making hours feel like days and days feel like mere moments. The sterile and tranquil atmosphere of the ward is a contrasting blend of healing and suffering, a place where time seems to stand still. Amid this paradox, I, Ethan, am navigating a journey of physical and emotional recuperation.

This morning, while I am wrestling with the task of consuming the bland, gelatinous hospital oatmeal, a flicker of movement at the door of my new room catches my attention. Standing in the doorway is a figure, backlit by the pale morning light filtering through the small window at the end of the hall. Guessing a couple of years older than me, his hair is a disheveled mass of dark curls, his eyes the vibrant blue of morning skies. His body is thin, almost fragile, but he carries himself with a certain dignity and strength.

"Hey," he greets me. His voice is a soothing baritone, as comforting and familiar as a distant song playing softly in the background.

Caught off guard, I manage to stammer out a response. "Hi."

Only then do I notice the network of scars on his arms. They stand out, raw and fierce, a testament to battles fought and endured. His gentle demeanour seems in stark contrast to the harsh evidence of his past struggles.

Observing my gaze, he offers a wry smile and makes his way across the room to sit in the vacant chair by my bedside. "Not the best conversation starter, I know," he comments.

I hurriedly shake my head, feeling a wave of embarrassment colour my cheeks. "I didn't mean to...I'm sorry."

He shrugs, seemingly unfazed by my scrutiny. "Don't be. We're all here for a reason, aren't we?"

There's a disarming honesty to his words, something that invites me to lower my defences a bit.

"I'm Alex," he offers, extending his hand towards me.

"Ethan," I respond, taking his hand in mine. The warmth of his skin contrasts with the cool, clinical sterility of the hospital room.

We sit in silence for a while, the quietude of the room occasionally interrupted by the distant beep of machines and the muffled sounds of nurses moving about in the hallway. Despite the circumstances, the silence is surprisingly comfortable, and I find myself enjoying his company.

"You're new here, right?" Alex asks after a while, his gaze studying me in a way that causes my heart to flutter unexpectedly.

I swallow, nodding in confirmation. "A few days, yeah."

He hums thoughtfully in response, filling the silence with a soft, contemplative sound. "Well, if you ever need someone to guide you through the ins and outs of this place, I'm your guy."

As I study him, I can't help but see a kindred spirit in

Alex. Like me, he is a traveler on a difficult path, bearing his scars with grace and courage. His morning-sky eyes and his raw strength, wrapped in vulnerability, have suddenly entered my new hospital room and my life, offering not just assistance, but also a glimmer of hope.

"Thank you, Alex," I say, managing a genuine smile for the first time in what feels like ages.

"No problem, Ethan," he responds, his eyes crinkling at the corners in a warm smile.

Opening up has never been my strong suit. For most of my life, books have been my sanctuary, my escape. The written word has always provided me with an opportunity to travel to different worlds where I could take on any identity, experience an array of emotions, and yet remain ensconced in a bubble of anonymity. However, here, within the sterile confines of the hospital, and in the company of Alex, who is navigating a path strikingly similar to mine, I sense an unprecedented shift stirring within myself.

The first thing Alex decides to share is a detailed story about his scars. There's a brief moment of stillness in the room, then a hint of a smile flickers across his face, suggesting a critical decision has been made. With an air of quiet resolve, he gently lifts his hospital gown, unveiling a constellation of scars scattered across his skin. Each scar differs in size and intensity, each one a silent testament to his tenacity and survival.

"So..." he begins, his voice low and calm. His fingers lightly trace over the embossed patterns on his skin with a detached, reverential air. His eyes, however, are not seeking out mine; instead, they remain focused on the physical reminders of his past battles.

"This one, I call Orion," he points to a particularly harsh scar stretching from his ribcage to his hip. His tone is almost affectionate, "This one reminds me of the hunter in the constellation. This is my trophy from when my kidneys decided to stage a mutiny." Despite the gravity of his revelation, his tone is laced with an unexpected note of humour, a subtle defiance against the solemnity of his circumstances.

His narrative continues to unfold naturally, like a stream flowing steadily, filling the room with its raw honesty. He moves on to identify the smallest scar on his body, a minuscule mark near his elbow. "This one's from a biopsy when they first discovered I was ill. It's almost unnoticeable, but this is where my life took a drastic turn; this was my personal Big Bang."

As he delves deeper into his journey with a life-threatening illness, his trials, and tribulations, his voice maintains a steady cadence. There's a sense of acceptance in his tone, an understanding that life can be harsh, yet it also harbours the potential for unparalleled beauty. He recounts the countless hospital visits, the numerous surgeries he has endured, the cycles of aggressive medications he's had to consume, and the physical pain that has been his constant companion, all with a level of grace that is truly astonishing.

According to him, each scar is more than just a symbol of the physical battles he has fought. They are also a tribute to his emotional resilience, a reminder of his inherent strength. They are the badges of his victories and defeats, a tangible representation of his courage, and his unwavering determination.

"And this one," he moves his fingers lightly to a larger, relatively fresh scar on his chest, "this one is Cassiopeia, the queen of constellations. I got this after a significant surgery a few months back. It was a close shave with death, but just like the queen, I didn't surrender."

His words resonate with an undeniable force, painting a vivid picture of his battle against the insidious clutches of death, yet his demeanour remains disarmingly casual. His voice is steady, calm, as if he is recounting a mundane event and not a life-defining struggle. There's a sense of power in his acceptance, an incredible ability to transform his personal struggles into engaging stories, and his scars into celestial constellations.

Despite the stark pain that is etched into every word he utters, there's a resilience in Alex that is both inspiring and humbling. In this shared moment of profound connection, I find an overwhelming urge welling up within me—an urge to reciprocate his honesty, to share a piece of my own journey, just as he has done.

And so, I find myself telling my own story, about the quiet corners where I found solace with my books, about the bustling hallways of school where I perpetually felt like an outsider peering in, about my quiet corner where I had come face-to-face with fear in its most terrifying form.

As my words fill the room, a rush of buried emotions break free: fear, loneliness, confusion. But amidst these tumultuous emotions, I also feel something else, something entirely unexpected—a sense of relief. It feels as though, for the first time in my life, someone is genuinely listening, seeing me for who I truly am, and not for who they want or expect me to be.

In this space of shared vulnerability, the sterile hospital room transforms into an intimate sanctuary. Words flow freely, serving as both a balm and a revelatory force. Here we are, two broken individuals, trying to find solace, understanding, and acceptance within each other's stories.

With every shared tale, the bond between us solidifies. Each sentence we speak, each pause we take, each emotive phrase we utter becomes an invisible thread that ties us together: the introverted bookworm and the resilient, candid patient. The conversation stretches on for hours, our voices harmonising with the rhythmic beep of machines and the sporadic hustle and bustle of the hospital ward.

As I lay bare my deepest fears, my doubts, and the emotional turmoil that comes with accepting my sexuality, Alex's expression remains unchanging. His gaze holds mine—encouraging, supportive—as if he understands the magnitude of my revelation. The judgement I had been dreading is conspicuously absent in his eyes. In its place, there's a silent understanding, a shared acknowledgment of the unique challenges that come with being different.

Through his stories, I am offered a rare glimpse into his world, into the struggles that have come to define him. And as he lays bare the chapters of his life, something within me resonates powerfully with his courage, his acceptance, his unwavering resolve. It's in this moment of profound connection that I realise, Alex and I, we are not as different as I had originally thought. We are both warriors, each battling our own adversities, each bearing our own scars, healing our own wounds, and attempting to navigate the unpredictable tumult that life often thrusts upon us.

In sharing our narratives, we find a sense of solace within each other. We find understanding and acceptance in the midst of pain and confusion. And in doing so, we embark on the journey towards healing, towards unravelling the complexities of our lives, one story at a time.

In the hushed silence of the hospital room, amidst the rhythmic beeping of machines and the soft rustling of curtains, Alex and I find a haven. A safe space where we can be our authentic selves, where we can wear our scars with pride.

As the cloak of nightfall settles over the hospital, a faint glow from the street lamps seeps through the half-shut blinds, gently illuminating our — now — shared room. I find myself wide awake, my mind tangled in a whirlwind of thoughts, while Alex's rhythmic breathing indicates his journey into the realm of dreams. Casting a glance at his form, I notice the interplay of shadow and light on the stark hospital walls, painting a silent story of resilience.

"Alex, are you awake?" I softly break the tangible silence, barely above a whisper.

A muffled "Hmm?" serves as his response, pulling him from his restful state.

"I can't sleep. Mind if we talk?..."

A brief pause ensues, followed by the rustling of sheets as he shifts in his adjacent bed. "Of course, Ethan. What's on your mind?"

"I don't know..." I falter, feeling a rush of vulnerability, "my fears, perhaps. And dreams."

I could almost envision the comforting curve of his usual smile. "Ah, the timeless human predicament," he muses, a soft chuckle lacing his words. "Very well, let's delve into our deepest fears and wildest dreams."

As silence swallows our words, I draw in a deep breath, my mind teetering on the precipice of fears I've kept buried. Words stumble and collide, struggling to form coherent sentences around the lump in my throat. Alex's patient reassurance, a whispered "You can start anywhere, Ethan," serves as the gentle nudge I need to topple over the edge of my silence.

"I'm...I'm terrified of returning to school," I confess, my voice wavering like a fragile thread on the brink of snapping. "Those unforgiving hallways, the sharp glances, the whispering echoes of judgment. The dread of standing at my locker, the fear of them...of the bullies, hunting me down." As my words fill the room, a tremor finds its way into my voice, but I press on, "I feel like I'm trapped in a perpetual nightmare, powerless to awaken."

With the room heavy with my confession, I steal a glance at Alex. His silhouette remains quiet, his attention unwavering. Encouraged by his silent support, I gather my strength to voice a fear even more daunting, more personal.

"Even though I've shared my secret with you, Alex, I'm still afraid," I continue, my heart echoing loudly in the silent room. "I've let out the truth that I've kept hidden for so long, yet it feels like a monstrous entity threatening to dismantle the fragile peace of my life. I...I'm terrified of what the world will make of who I truly am."

In the sanctuary of the night, my admission feels equally frightening and liberating. The silence stretches thin as I hold my breath, waiting for a reaction, rejection, comfort, anything. From the shadowy figure across the room, I receive only patience, devoid of judgment, fuelling my courage to confront the truth that has remained shrouded for too long.

As silence embraces us, I finally hear, calm and gentle, cutting through my turmoil, "Thank you, Ethan, for entrusting me with your fears. As I see it, your identity isn't something to fear, but rather something to embrace with pride. But I understand your distress in the face of everything that happened."

Talking to him I always feel a genuine understanding, a form of acceptance... His sincere words doesn't eliminate all my fears, but it lights a spark of hope in the shadowy recesses of my mind.

After a beat of silence, Alex assumes the mantle of the confessor. His voice, typically vibrant with life and humour, now carries a somber note.

"I live in fear of my disease, Ethan," he begins, his soft words laden with undeniable weight, filling the silent room.

"Each day is a battlefield. Every morning I confront the uncertainty of whether today will be the day my body succumbs, the day I lose."

The heaviness of his words is palpable, a stark contrast to his habitual optimism.

"But what terrifies me more," he carries on, his voice teetering on the brink of audibility, "is the prospect of succumbing to death without ever truly experiencing life."

He allows the words to linger, giving them the gravity they deserve. A pang of empathy resonates within me. Here is Alex, still in the spring of life, confronting mortality with a poise and depth that belies his years.

"I see people outside, navigating the dance of life, falling in love, making mistakes, crafting memories... and I... I am confined to this sterile hospital bed, watching the world evolve through a glass barrier," he confesses, a hint of bitterness tainting his words.

His raw vulnerability pierces the silence, and the barriers around his emotions collapse, revealing the profound sorrow in his heart. But amidst the fear and the grief, I see a hint of acceptance, a willingness to confront his fears, to persevere despite them.

"I often ponder - have I truly lived?" he says, his gaze lost in the night sky across the window. "Have I loved sufficiently, laughed heartily, made an impact? Will I leave behind a story that resonates, or will I merely be another name in a hospital ledger?"

His words echo in the room, carrying an undercurrent of regret and unfulfilled desires. But beneath it all, they reveal a fierce determination - a resolve to defy his fears, to seize every moment, and to leave a legacy that endures.

As the dense weight of our fears begins to lift, we traverse into the realm of dreams. The atmosphere subtly shifts, becoming less oppressive, yet retaining its intensely personal aura.

"You know, I've always loved books," I start, "They've been my sanctuary, my getaway. But they've also shaped my dreams."

Alex absorbs my words, his gaze soft, prompting me to delve deeper. I take a calming breath, gathering my scattered thoughts. "One day, I aspire to become an author," I admit, the words tasting unfamiliar as they cross my lips, given I've rarely shared this dream before.

"A storyteller," I elaborate, a newfound steadiness creeping into my voice. "I aim to sculpt worlds, Alex. Worlds that offer solace to anyone who seeks it, much like how I've found refuge in mine. Worlds that embrace you, irrespective of who you are."

"I desire to populate them with characters," I continue, the corners of my mouth curving into a smile at the prospect. "People who embody authenticity, who are beautifully flawed, who evolve. I yearn to document journeys, growth, and love in all its varied forms."

"And the narratives," I add, excitement fluttering within me. "I aspire to craft tales that evoke emotions, that provoke contemplation. Stories that comfort and confront, that fracture hearts and then knit them back together. Stories that reflect society, yet also illuminate the path towards acceptance and love."

I pause, allowing my dreams to permeate the room. They seem more tangible now, more attainable than ever before. Voicing them to Alex, in this hushed hospital room, feels akin to taking the first stride towards their manifestation. Speaking them into existence, it seems, lends them power, brings them to life.

"Dreams are so personal, aren't they" Alex murmurs after a beat, his voice brimming with admiration. "They grant us something to strive for, to hope for. And your dream, Ethan, it's truly captivating."

His acknowledgement, his comprehension, imbues me with a sensation of truly being seen. And in that fleeting moment, under the dim hospital lights, our dreams intertwine, cementing a bond that feels as solid as the earth beneath us. This marks the genesis of an understanding, a tacit vow to support each other's dreams, regardless of their magnitude or complexity.

After the silent affirmation of our shared aspirations, Alex's gaze drifts away, focusing on the sterile hospital walls. The silence stretches, seemingly mustering the strength to encapsulate his dreams. And when he finally voices them, his words exude a straightforward profundity, a characteristic uniquely his.

"All I yearn for is to live, Ethan," he begins, his voice surprisingly firm. His gaze remains affixed to the wall, as if the bland, off-white surface unlocked a world he yearned to explore. "It might sound cliché, but given my circumstances, living itself is a dream."

He redirects his gaze towards me, his eyes reflecting the resolve in his voice. "I yearn to explore the world," he presses on, each word ringing with increasing conviction. "To tread upon unfamiliar paths, sample unpronounceable cuisines, witness the sunrise from a distant horizon."

There's a sincerity to his voice that makes me hang onto his every word. He speaks of yearning for love and reciprocation, of the desire to experience the thrilling flush of romance, the soothing warmth of affection.

"And age," he appends, almost as an afterthought. "I desire the opportunity to complain about an aching back, to witness my hair silvering, to observe the world evolving."

The gravity of his words, the depth of his longing for experiences most take for granted, strikes a chord. It isn't about lofty dreams or extraordinary achievements; it's about the everyday moments that constitute life.

However, his dreams are not moulded by his disease. Instead, they're carved by his spirit, a spirit ready to accept life in all its uncertainties and surprises. His dream is about choosing to embrace life, whatever it may bring, and by sharing it, Alex presents a picture of resilience, fortitude, and a yearning for the ordinary beauty of life.

"Dreams are personal, aren't they?" Alex muses, his eyes shimmering in the dim light. "They're fragments of us, extensions of our hopes, our desires. Even when life pushes us to the edge, we don't abandon our dreams. We clutch onto them, because that's all we can do."

The gravity of his words settles into the ensuing silence. His dreams, like his stories, are etched into his essence, and sharing them feels as intimate and sacred as a confession. It is this shared vulnerability that binds our dreams together, reinforcing the connection that is beginning to form between us. As our dialogue continues, a connection solidifies, a bond birthed from shared vulnerabilities and dreams.

As the night deepens, our conversation gradually ebbs, replaced by our introspective silences. Lying there in my hospital bed, I find myself in uncharted waters. Feelings for Alex are budding within me, emotions I am fearful to confront, yet unable to dismiss. The anxiety tied to my identity, my secret, resurfaces, complicating the maze of my thoughts further.

However, in this moment, under the faint glow of the lights from the window, with Alex's steady breaths lulling me to sleep, I allow myself to dream - a dream where fears are surmountable, secrets are tolerable, and maybe, just maybe, I could let myself explore the bewildering emotions blossoming within me.

Our discussion about fears and dreams transcends a mere

nocturnal conversation. It serves as a window into our souls, a bond being forged. This night is laden with revelations and realisations, and as I finally succumb to sleep, I can't help but perceive it as a turning point for both Alex and me. This hospital haven, our shared respite, is gradually transforming into a place of understanding and acceptance - a refuge amidst our personal tempests.

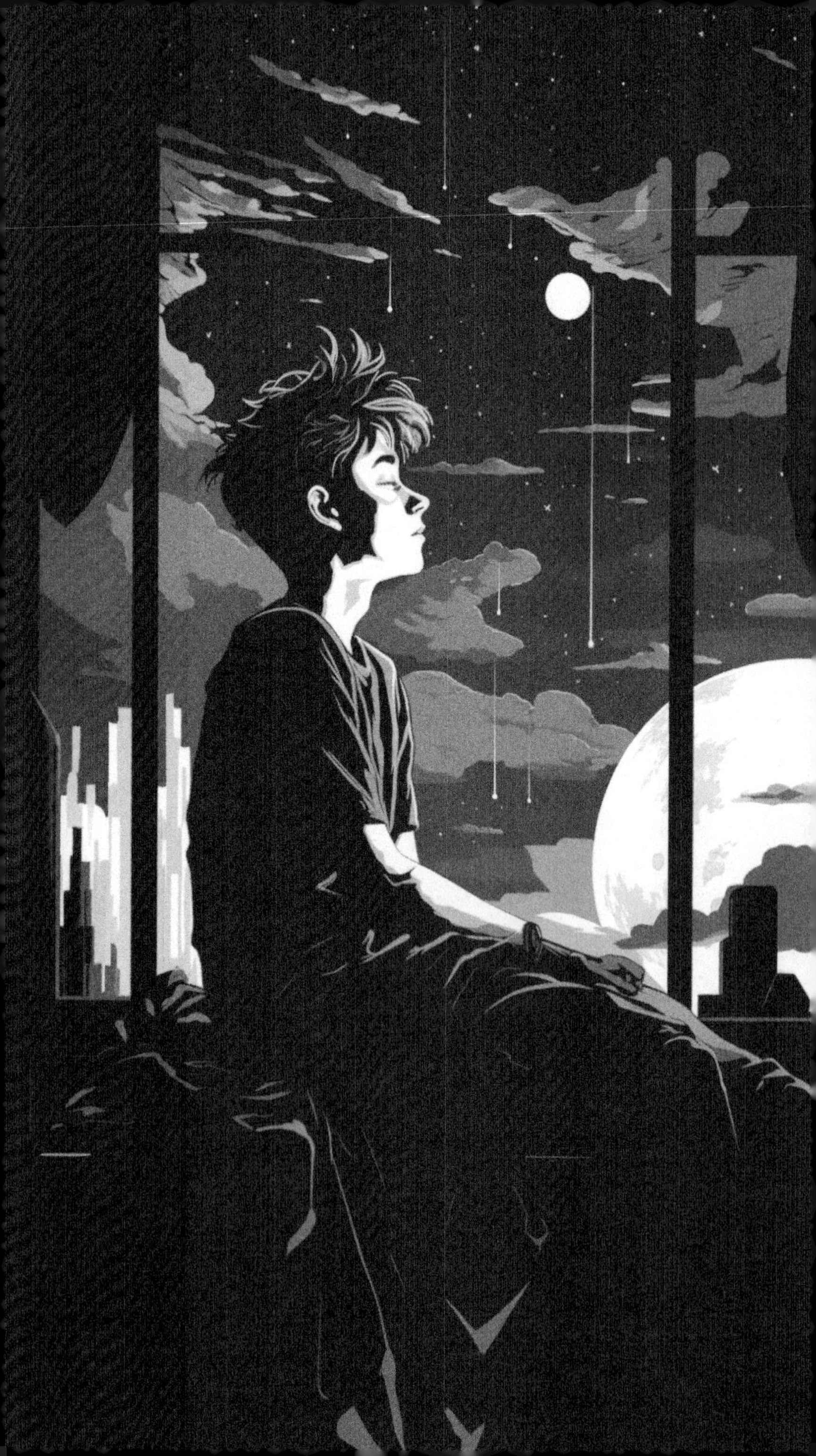

4
WINDOW TALKS

The morning light slips into the hospital room, creating a kind of gentle glow. It's almost like the universe is giving me a thumbs up, recognising how much last night changed things. That conversation with Alex, laying it all out there – our dreams, our fears – it's like I'm a different person now.

I look at Alex, sound asleep. His chest moves up and down, steady and peaceful, a small smile stuck on his face. A wave of relief washes over me, strange but welcome. Opening up, sharing things I've never dared say out loud before, and getting acceptance instead of judgement – it's freeing.

It's an awesome feeling, knowing that someone sees you, the real you. I've spent so much of my life hiding behind fear and doubt, scared of what might happen if I showed my true self. But here in this hospital room, with its constant hum of machines and steady heart monitor beeps, I've started on a journey to accepting myself.

Something draws me to the window, the outside world calling me. The sky is clear, the morning sun bathing the city in a golden light. Life goes on, just like it always does. Streets are busy with cars and people, everyone caught up in their own world. Among all this normal chaos, I find a strange sense of peace.

On my journey to figure myself out, in my struggle, I'm not alone. There are others out there just like me, fighting their fears, chasing their dreams. We're all living different lives, facing different problems, but there's one thing we share – the journey of understanding and accepting who we are.

I turn back to Alex. His steady breathing, the calm he's radiating, it underlines the connection we've built. We're both navigating our own storms, but through our shared experiences, we've found a guiding light in each other.

Taking a deep breath, I take in the calm morning, the comforting presence of Alex. It feels like the start of something new, a small but important step in my journey. For the first time, I feel like I'm moving forward. In this quiet moment of acceptance, I know I'm ready to face whatever comes my way. Because in the end, I can be imperfect and scared, but definitely me. And that's enough. It has to be.

Our days in the hospital have a routine now. Alex and I, we get through each day with words and looks that say more than they should, and every passing moment pulls us closer.

Our world is this hospital, all white walls and beeping machines, and a never-ending line of nurses and doctors. It's a strange place to call home, but in this weird world, we've found a friendship that's just as strange and just as beautiful.

We chat about everything and nothing, crack jokes under the too-bright hospital lights, and keep each other company when the nights are too long and sleep won't come. There's a bond there, forged through the crazy stuff we're going through, and every shared word, every shared silence makes it stronger.

Alex is... He's something else. He's taught me more about

life and myself than I thought I could learn in a hospital. I'm drawn to his strength, his ability to smile despite the crappy hand life's dealt him. His positivity, even when he's fighting a disease that scares the hell out of me, is kinda amazing.

Talking with him is like diving into a cool book, the kind that just keeps getting better the more you read. Every chat is a new page, a new chapter, and the more I get to know Alex, the more I respect him.

I remember this one afternoon, just after we'd come back from more tests. Alex, as usual, was handling everything like a champ, smiling at me as we got back to our room.

"You're okay, Ethan?" he asked, looking at me like he could see right through me.

"Yeah, I'm good," I told him, smiling back. Moments like these, when we look out for each other, it really hits me how much our friendship means.

That night, we ate in silence. But it wasn't a weird silence, it was comfortable, reassuring. We didn't need words to know we had each other's back.

After dinner, we sat by the window, our usual spot, with Alex's favourite song playing softly. It's become part of our routine now.

Sitting here, watching the world outside, I thought about how much things had changed. I came to this hospital scared and confused, but thanks to Alex, I'm starting to see things differently, to see myself differently.

Looking at him, bathed in moonlight, he catches my eye and gives me a smile that makes everything feel a bit better.

That's when it hits me - He isn't just another patient or a buddy; he is my guiding light in this storm. I realise how important he has become to me. I've changed since I've been here, and a lot of it is thanks to him. As I sit there, thinking about everything, I feel pretty grateful for it all - the hospital, the journey, and especially Alex.

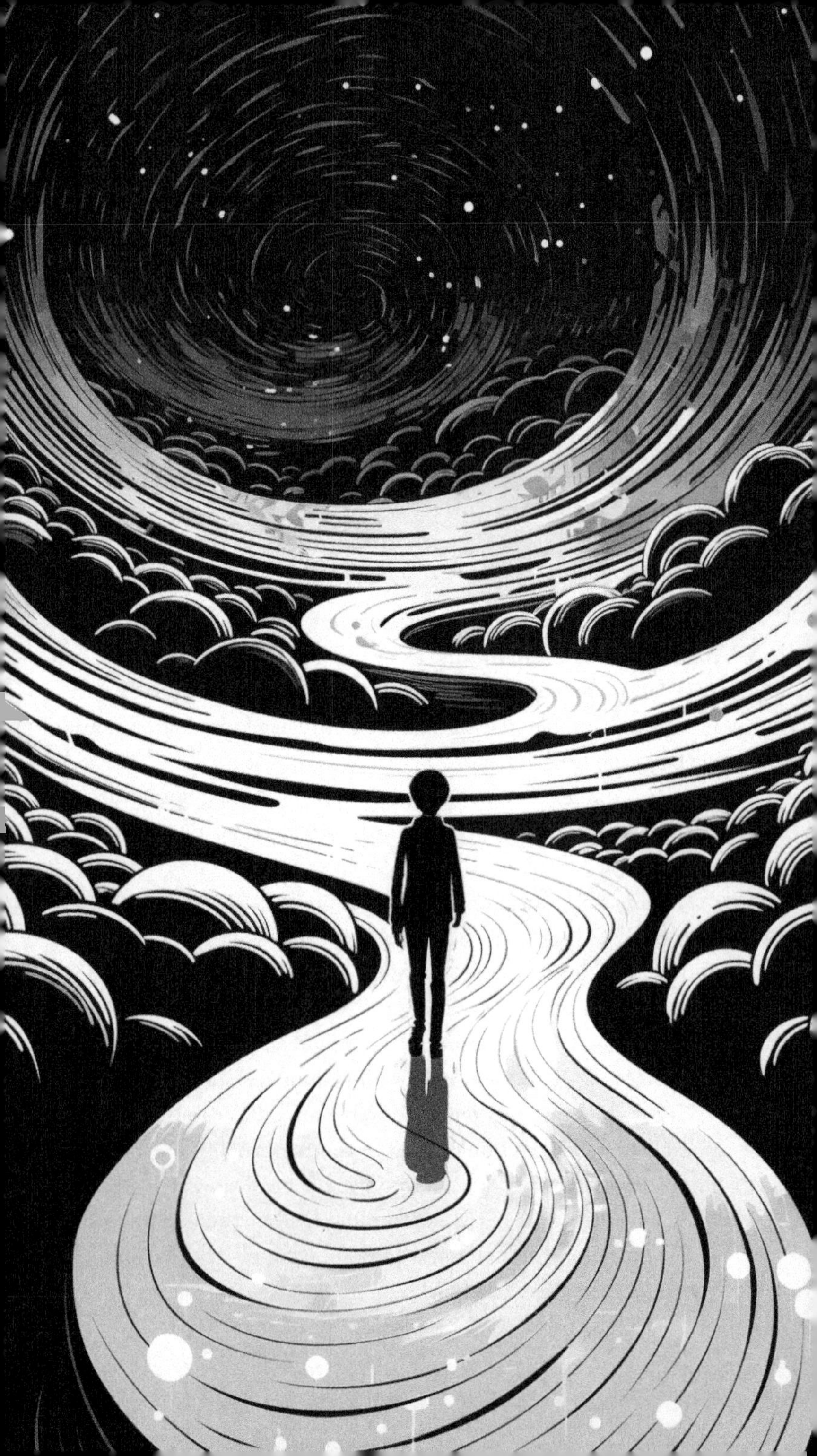

5
THE LONG WALK HOME

Dr. Jensen's declaration of my impending discharge triggers a torrent of emotions within me. The antiseptic white walls of the hospital, once symbolic of my confinement, have gradually transformed into a haven. A cocoon insulating me from the ruthless truths of the outside world. Here, I've been allowed to be me, free from fear or judgment. Yet now, I stand on the precipice of leaving this sanctuary.

As the sun descends beneath the horizon, painting the sky in hues of crimson and gold, I perch on the edge of my hospital bed, lost in thought. The room reverberates with a disquieting silence in the absence of Alex's buoyant laughter. He's been transferred to another wing for intensive therapy. His absence accentuates my solitude, a bitter preview of the isolation waiting for me at home.

The hospital's predictable routine has evolved into my lifeline. Here, I am not the 'odd one out,' not a pariah. I am simply Ethan. The idea of departing from this safe bubble stirs a nagging disquiet in my core.

I peer out the window, the outside world appearing

remote, unfamiliar. The steady throbbing of my heart echoes the ticking of the wall clock, each tick nudging me closer to my impending exit. Night engulfs the world outside, a thick blanket of darkness dotted with the distant glow of city lights. The silence, intermittently punctuated by the rustle of the wind or an echoing hum from the hospital corridors, is suffocating.

Fear slithers into my thoughts, painting unnerving images of what lies ahead. Recognisable judgmental glares, school hallways filled with murmured whispers, lurking bullies. The dread of facing all this again is crippling.

As I recline on the bed, the softness of hospital sheets, the underlying tang of disinfectant, and the muted chatter of nurses outside merge into my consciousness. All of it feels familiar, soothing in an odd way.

However, a part of me pines for home. The scent of mom's homemade cookies wafting through the air, the permeating echoes of dad's vintage rock records in the living room, the comfort of my own bed. Home, with its familiar warmth, beckons me, promising a return to regularity, an opportunity to retrieve my hijacked life.

But, the home I'm returning to, the person I've become, is irrevocably changed.

Ensnared in this emotional tug-of-war, relief grapples with anxiety, and exhilaration jousts with fear. I teeter on the edge of a pivotal life chapter, preparing to dive headlong into the great unknown.

Moonlight filters through the window, casting elongated, ghostly shadows on the hospital floor. I think of Alex. His unwavering spirit, infectious optimism, his acceptance. I ruminate on our shared moments, stories, dreams. I understand that although I'm leaving this place, I'm taking a piece of it with me. The resilience, courage, acceptance I've found here – they've become woven into the fabric of my being.

With this revelation, a flicker of determination flares to life within me. The world outside, with its jagged edges shimmering with judgment and hostility, looms menacingly. But the trembling, lonesome boy who once would've shrunk back now stands firm, his backbone tempered by the trials of this journey. Strength courses through my veins where fear once dominated, bravery flexing its newfound prowess. The thought of facing the world, of confronting my own reflection, no longer triggers an instinct to flee. Instead, it rings the bell for a match I'm now ready to fight.

I shut my eyes, inhaling deeply. Anxiety and fear remain, but instead of escaping them, I invite them in. I recognise the challenging path that lies ahead but also acknowledge that I'm not treading it solo.

For the first time in what feels like forever, I find myself eager for the journey, the long walk home.

***

As dawn begins its ascent, I stir from sleep. The hospital room pulses with a new kind of energy today, charged with the burden of impending change. Every noise, every movement—rustling sheets, zipping up my bag, the echo of shoes against the cold floor—seems magnified, each bringing me a step closer to the dividing line of farewell, a moment filled with dread and expectation.

Alex is already awake when I step into his room. Propped up in bed, he wears a gentle smile, his gaze fixed on the world outside the window. An envelope of stillness encases us, punctured only by the sporadic song of a bird. The morning sun casts ethereal light in his eyes, giving him an almost alien beauty.

"Good morning," he says, his voice sturdy despite the glint of sorrow in his gaze.

"Morning," I respond, straining to mirror his poise. My heart is a wild drum, my palms slick with sweat.

A weighted silence falls, thick with unspoken sentiments, impending goodbyes, and the sting of separation.

"This is it," I finally manage to murmur. Speaking it aloud morphs the thought into a tangible reality, intensifying the ache.

He nods, his gaze unwavering, his voice composed yet charged with emotion.

"Ethan," he starts, his tone both tender and firm, "This isn't our end."

"But, I'm leaving," I interrupt, disappointment tinging my voice.

"You'll return. You'll visit me," he insists, locking his gaze with mine.

"But it won't be the same," I counter, my words weighted with emotion.

"No, it won't," he admits, a ghost of a smile on his lips. "But change isn't always bad. It's just different."

Staring at Alex, my beacon of sanity amidst the bedlam, my guiding star in the consuming darkness, I realise he's right. Change isn't an innate demon. Sure, it's scary, but it's also essential. Necessary for growth, evolution, survival.

"I'll miss you, Ethan," he whispers.

"I'll miss you too, Alex," I reply, the words heavy in my throat.

We spend the following minutes in silence, simply being in each other's presence, drawing comfort from our shared silence, our bond.

As the time to leave draws near, I draw a deep breath, etching his image in my memory—his tousled hair, bright eyes, radiant smile. My friend, my confidant, my rock.

I step forward, pulling him into a fierce hug. An embrace interlaced with gratitude, yearning, and goodbye. He reciprocates, his arms offering a solid refuge. For a fleeting moment, the world falls away. It's just him and me, encapsulated in our bubble.

Stepping back, I whisper, "Thank you, Alex."

"For what?" he asks, surprise in his eyes.

"For everything," I answer, my voice thick with feeling.

Exiting his room, I look back one last time. There's Alex, smiling softly, his eyes a mirror of promise—a vow of friendship that defies time and distance, a bond resilient in the face of adversity, a connection unbreakable.

My parents are waiting for me in the hallway when I step out of Alex's room. They offer comforting smiles, their understanding silence a balm for my raw emotions.

As I walk away from the hospital, my parents on either side of me, I understand this isn't a goodbye, but a 'see you soon'. A pledge of a future where we'll reconvene, our bond will grow, our friendship will prosper.

Every step on the long journey home doesn't echo with sorrow or fear but resonates with a silent symphony of hope, expectation, dreams. The town's familiar sights and sounds, once mundane, now glisten with newfound life and promise. My parents and I talk little during the walk home, our conversation meandering through everyday topics, an attempt to reclaim normalcy.

A breeze carries the scent of blooming flowers, awakening my senses with the perfume of fresh starts. I notice my shoulders settling a little higher, the past's heaviness feeling a tad lighter.

I trace the veins on my hands, the same hands that once clung to hospital sheets, now ready to embrace the world. The reflections in shop windows no longer capture a timid, uncertain Ethan, but a transformed me—a figure standing taller, with eyes holding not just reflection but determination.

Instead of shying away from the street's humdrum, I find

myself moving in sync with life's rhythmic dance, prepared to embrace existence on my terms. The world outside the hospital isn't a war zone to conquer but a stage to play my role, not with fear but with courage and authenticity.

When we finally reach home, I feel a sense of readiness, a readiness to face the challenges and live life on my terms. As I step through the door, the echo of its closing sounds not like a chapter ending, but like a new one beginning.

Night descends as I sit in my room, my fingers brushing the sharp corners of textbooks that have gathered dust during my hiatus. A knot of apprehension tightens in my throat; my once familiar sanctuary morphs into a purgatory, the outside world brimming with stark, daunting realities. School, the gladiator pit of my unease and harassment, lurks at the break of dawn.

A glance in the mirror reveals a different Ethan staring back. A new determination flickers in my eyes, an outline of resilience contours my features, invisible yet palpable. I'm altered, matured, advanced. Will they see this transformation? The tormentors who once revealed in my despair, the spectators who observed in silence, the teachers who favoured ignorance over action?

As I turn the pages of my textbooks, the typically soothing scent of paper and ink barely quells the internal tumult. Will they recall the meek Ethan they once derided, or will they see a reborn individual, someone who has learned to accept himself, someone blessed with a friend like Alex?

The silence of my room amplifies each tick of the wall clock, a reminder of the rapidly closing gap to the inevitable morning, the looming showdown with school. This thought summons a tidal wave of trepidation. What if their view of me remains stagnant? What if I'm still the prime target?

However, amidst these waves, a glimmer of hope exists, a tiny flame stoked by Alex's words and resilience. I revisit our nocturnal conversations, our shared dreams, our exchanged smiles, and the fortitude we drew from each other. Alex, despite facing life's harsh realities, had summoned the audacity to defy them. His words, "Change isn't always bad. It's just different," resonate within me.

"Different," once a label, a source of agony, an emblem of alienation, now possesses a new interpretation. It's an honour badge, an indication of resilience, a symbol of acceptance.

That night, sleep carries me into a dreamscape where fear and anticipation for the forthcoming day coexist. School, with its lengthy corridors, teeming classrooms, and chorus of chatter, is vivid in my dream. But here, I stride those hallways with an uplifted chin, courage in my gaze. Smiles, acceptance, respect greet me. It's a dream, certainly, but also a mirror reflecting the reality I crave, the metamorphosis I anticipate.

***

THE MORNING SUN BATHES MY ROOM, ITS SOFT RAYS dancing on the walls. A new day, a new dawn, and with it, a fresh wave of jitters. But beneath the frosty tendrils of fear, a spark of confidence glows, echoing a vow made in a hospital room, testament to the power of friendship.

The weight of the school bag on my shoulder doesn't feel burdensome anymore; rather, it feels like a backpack of bravery. It signifies not just the scholastic knowledge I carry, but also the personal wisdom I've garnered. It's weighty, but each gram narrates a tale of transformation, growth, and acceptance.

As I exit my home, the familiar route leading to school unfurls before me, uncertain yet welcoming. Each stride I take pulsates with purpose, every footfall a declaration of my determination. The journey may be arduous and the road uneven, but every step takes me closer to a future radiant with possibilities – brighter, bolder, and pregnant with promise.

The reflection of the boy in the hospital seems remote now. I remain Ethan, but an Ethan transformed. Within me, I carry not just strength, but valour; not just acceptance, but pride. I'm primed, ready to confront the world that once brought me to my knees, ready to challenge the obstacles that once appeared insurmountable. I've navigated the labyrinth of fear and emerged on the other side.

The morning chill nips at me, standing stark against the formidable structure of my school. Faces I'm used to seeing appear, faces that used to brew a gnarly mix of unease and anxiety within me. They all swivel in my direction as I approach, expressions blooming with surprise and curiosity. But there's something different in their stares, an odd unfamiliarity, an unexplored gap that wasn't there before.

Winding my way through the labyrinthine hallways of the school, the whispers that follow me are unrelenting, like ghostly echoes. Their words press heavy on me, thick with rumour and intrigue. Unresolved questions hang in the air like a song left unfinished – why was Ethan hospitalised? What happened? And most importantly, who was behind it?

Honesty is my usual game, except for this one lie that slipped out too easily—I claimed a foggy memory of the incident, the identities of the culprits lost in a mist of torment and terror. The cold fact is, I remember every detail, every second of that hellish day. The faces, the derisive laughter, the hate-filled words are burned into my memory, along with the physical agony, the fear, and the shame. Yet, I chose to lock up this truth within me. Why? Because I was scared.

Scared of what might follow, scared of their retaliation, scared of being painted as a target once again. Above all, I was petrified of my secret coming to light. The attack wasn't some random act of violence; it was a hate crime, venomous revulsion aimed at me for being me, for being different, for being gay.

My parents, the police—they swallowed my lie whole. They accepted my pretend amnesia. It was easier that way, simpler for them to label it a random act of violence, and simpler for me to skirt around the harsh truth of homophobia.

But as the day marches on—through lessons, through brief nods to familiar faces—a gnawing sense of guilt and fear nibbles persistently at my conscience. Guilt for keeping silent, for not taking a stand. Fear of what lies ahead, of the truth threatening to burst forth.

Slipping away to the isolation of the school bathroom, I find myself staring at my reflection. I see a scared boy hiding behind a lie, a boy fighting to protect himself, his secret. But there's a glint of defiance in his eyes, a spark kindled by Alex's words, his courage.

"I need to stop living in fear," I whisper to the mirror image. Alex's bravery stirred me to face my fears, to challenge them. To truly honour our friendship, I must take these words to heart. I must be true to myself, to my experiences.

When the final bell tolls through the school, signalling the close of the day, I find myself at a juncture. The road ahead is daunting, filled with apprehension and uncertainty. But it's also a path of transformation. And I know what I must do.

I will no longer allow fear to gag me. I will speak up, share my story, confront my assailants. It won't be a cakewalk; I am all too aware. There will be fallout, challenges, hurdles. But I am ready to take them on, one day at a time. For myself, for Alex, for every other 'Ethan' out there living in shadows.

Stepping out of the school gate, an unusual sense of liberation sweeps over me, as if a hefty burden has been lifted from my chest. Sure, I am scared, but entwined with this fear is a sprouting hope. Hope for a world where I can be unapologetically me, where love is unprejudiced.

<hr />

SITTING IN OUR FAMILY DINING SPACE, AMID THE PLAYFUL laughter and rhythmic chime of silverware, I feel curiously detached. The friendly banter of my parents recounting their workday, their nonchalant curiosity about my inaugural day back at school, all feel eerily distant—like a fuzzy, muted film screening miles away. This is because my thoughts are elsewhere. My thoughts are with Alex.

His laughter, his tenacity, his infectious zeal for existence, had served as a lighthouse in my darkest era, a lifeline yanking me from the abyss of dread and self-disgust. Now, his absence carves a gaping void, and I wrestle with an unfamiliar type of terror—the trepidation stirred by my nascent feelings for him.

Each time I shutter my eyes, Alex surfaces. His beaming grin, his effervescent eyes, the crow's feet sketching appealing patterns on his face when he chuckles. I can discern his voice, a serene, reassuring melody that infused even the most tranquil moments with warmth and affection. His spirit, his very existence, seems to have saturated every pore of my being, anchoring itself within the fortress of my heart.

With every second that slips away, his absence amplifies. The yearning for him roars like an unbridled wildfire. I yearn to see him, listen to him, be in his proximity. This longing bewilders me, petrifies me even, as I've never traversed this emotional landscape before.

"Ethan, are you okay?" The thread of anxiety woven into my mom's inquiry jolts me back to the present.

I elevate my eyes to meet her compassionate gaze. "Yeah,

Mom, I'm okay," I assure her, managing a weak smile. Yet, my heart tightens, bombarded by thoughts of Alex.

Could it be? Am I tumbling headfirst into the abyss of love for Alex?

This revelation unleashes a tsunami of fear. It's not merely the acceptance of my sexuality that fuels this terror; it's the acknowledgment that I'm plummeting for a boy who has evolved into my anchor, my confidant, my ally. It's confronting the probability that my emotions for him could muddy the waters, could disrupt the equilibrium of our camaraderie.

But as the fear escalates, a flicker of hope, of anticipation, rises too. Because beneath the panic and befuddlement, I discern something profound, something tangible. A bond transcending friendship, a tie tempered by shared encounters and shared vulnerabilities.

A love that has blossomed in hushed interludes, in mutual laughter and tears, in shared dreams and apprehensions. A love as intimidating as it is consoling, as enigmatic as it is enlightening.

So, here I sit, amid the symphony of silverware and the hum of conversation, granting myself the permission to acknowledge this love. I allow myself to experience it, to embrace it. Because it's a fragment of me, of my journey, of my authenticity.

For the first time in a seemingly eternal stretch, I permit myself to nurture hope. Hope that maybe Alex echoes my sentiments. Hope that perhaps I could find solace in his arms. Hope that love might reign supreme.

❧

TOSSING AND SQUIRMING IN MY BED, I SENSE THE DAY'S residue of emotions concocting a tumultuous energy within me. The room is shrouded in darkness, the only glimmer of light comes from the ethereal glow of the moonlight seeping in through the window. It's as if the night mirrors my restlessness, dancing to the rhythm of my emotional upheaval.

The loneliness of my room accentuates the gaping hole that manifested with my reintroduction into reality, the world outside the comforting boundaries of the hospital and the solace provided by Alex's presence. It's the same room I've grown up in, the same walls that have observed my laughter and tears, but it feels alien now. Amid the stillness, in the heart of solitude, I yearn for Alex. I miss him in a way that gnaws at my core, a longing that fills my mind with images of him, of us.

The sudden buzz of my phone startles me, jolting me from my introspection. I fumble for the device on the bedside table, my heartbeat throbbing with expectation. As the screen springs to life, a wave of comfort washes over me at the sight of his name on the screen. Alex.

> I bet you're still awake

> I can't sleep either >.<

Another message swiftly follows.

> How was the big day?

My fingers freeze above the screen, my mind a whirlpool of thoughts. Should I reveal my uncertainties, the anxious shadow that's been tailing me all day? Should I admit the profound loneliness that's enveloped me since leaving the safety of the hospital, from him?

With a hefty sigh, I rake a hand through my hair. It's late, and the last thing I want is to offload my worries and doubts onto him.

> It was okay

> Different, but okay

I manage to type back, my fingers trembling slightly.

But as I hit send, a pang of guilt assaults me. Because it's not okay, not in the least. I'm scared, bewildered, lost at sea. And the only person who could anchor me, who could dispel my solitude, is miles apart.

Are u okay?

Alex's reply comes almost instantaneously. His concern, mere characters on a screen, injects a dose of warmth into my chest, tempering the icy dread gnawing at my insides.

> I'm just...

I halt, fingers hovering over the glowing screen. How can I convey the maelstrom of feelings raging inside me? How do I express the longing, the fear, the confusion?

> Missing you

I manage to tap out, my heart pounding against my ribcage. It's a risk, a stride into the unknown. But it's also the truth—a truth I need him to understand.

As the message sends, a wave of nervous energy overwhelms me. Will he get it? Does he reciprocate my feelings?

The seconds crawl by, each one stretching into infinity. The suspense tightens a knot in my gut, sends shivers coursing down my spine. And then, just when I'm ready to admit defeat, my phone vibrates.

> I miss you too, Ethan.
>
> More than you know...

The message is simple, but it conveys so much more. The words cocoon me like a warm blanket, a beacon in the cold, desolate night. It's a confirmation.

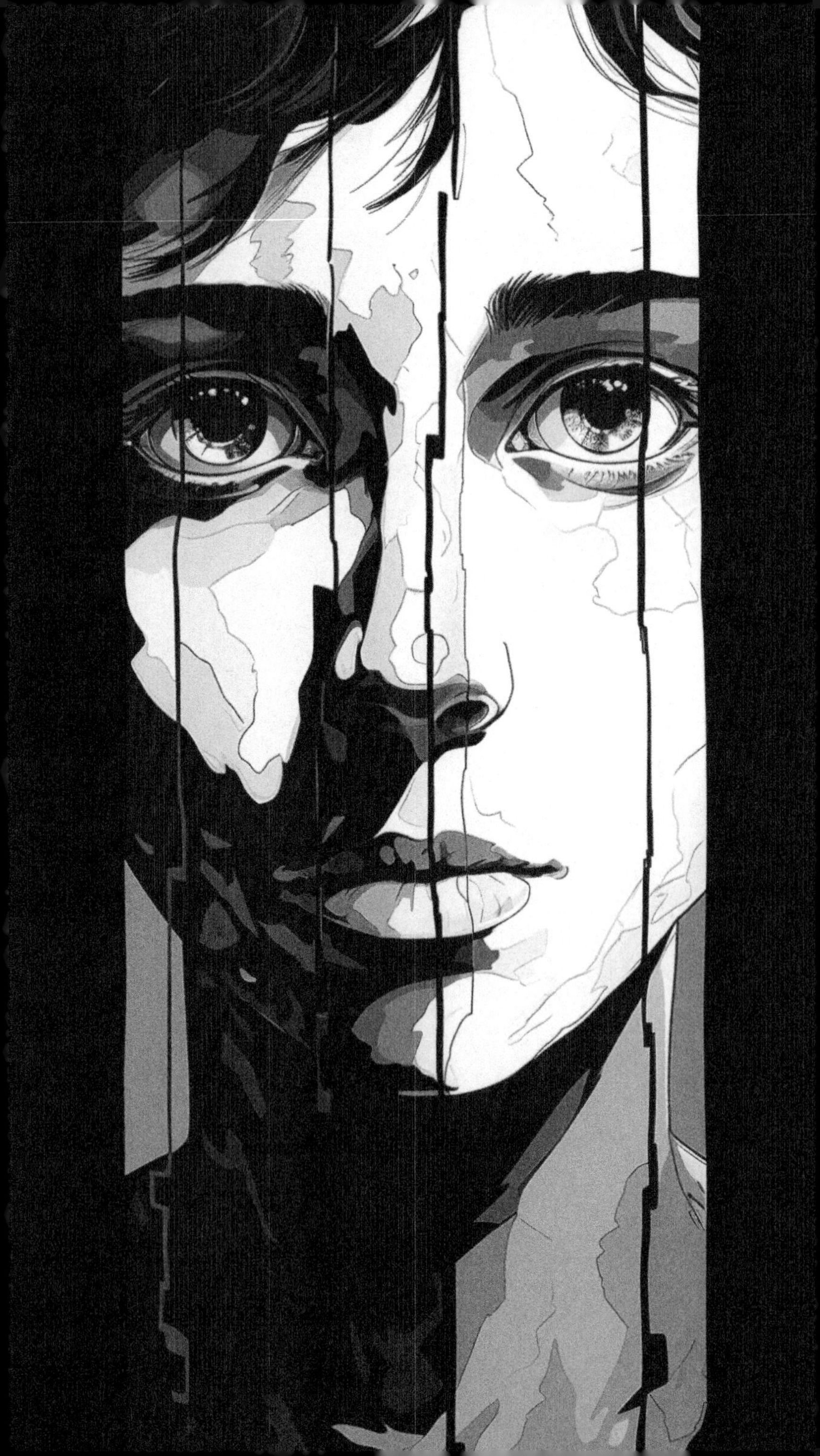

6
A NEW MIRROR

Standing in front of the mirror, I critically examine the figure returning my gaze. My reflection appears alien—a distant echo of the kid I once was, the boy I thought I was. The harsh fluorescent lights cast harsh shadows on my face, emphasising the under-eye bags and the vacant expression that has staked a permanent claim. The face in the mirror is mine, yet it feels unfamiliar, almost like an intruder's.

I lift a hand, making contact with the cool surface of the mirror. It's a strange feeling, witnessing oneself through one's own eyes. There's a disparity there—a divide between the person mirrored and the person you believe yourself to be.

The hospital stint, the incident, Alex—all have left their indelible mark on me. Not visible scars, unlike the ones that etch a map on Alex's skin, but marks all the same. They're invisible, hidden beneath the surface, deeply rooted within my psyche. Now, they're a part of me—woven into my story, my identity.

But then, what is my identity? Who am I, really?

For a lengthy period, I defined myself through the lens of

others. I was the quiet kid, the shy one, the bullies' punching bag. I was the evader, the secret bearer, the outlier. That was the image in the mirror, the projection I'd grown to accept as my identity.

But now, standing here, I realise that's not who I am. Not any longer.

My thoughts meander to Alex—his tenacity, his courage, his embrace of his identity. He wears his scars like badges of honour, with defiance. They're a testament to his struggles, his journey. They're a part of him, but they don't define him.

And perhaps, I can learn to be that way too.

I dwell on our late-night talks, our shared dreams, our connection. The fear, the confusion, the guilt that once swallowed me seem to recede, replaced by a quiet acceptance. Yes, I am different. My feelings for Alex are something I hadn't anticipated, something I can't quite wrap my head around. But that doesn't make them—or me—wrong.

Because, standing here, looking at my reflection, I understand something pivotal. My identity, my selfhood, isn't just a reflection of how others see me. It's not merely the cumulative result of my experiences. It's not dictated by my fears or my past.

No, my identity is uniquely mine. It's my emotions, my dreams, my hopes. It's the love I feel for Alex, the inner strength I've unearthed. It's my determination, my resilience, my ability to face my fears. It's the serene acceptance that has pushed the confusion aside, the peace that has supplanted guilt.

And as I stand there, studying my reflection, I feel an unusual wave of relief wash over me. Because, for the first time, I truly see myself. Not the image crafted by others, not the image sculpted by my fears, but the genuine me. The me who loves, who dreams, who hopes. The me who is brave, who is strong, who is unique...

THE IDEA OF COMING OUT IS AN EXHILARATING JUMBLE OF terror and liberation.

Perched on the edge of my bed, I pull my knees to my chest, my gaze lost on the opposite wall. My mind is a hurricane, thoughts swirling and crashing together into chaotic patterns of expectation, fear, and optimism. My heart pounds against my ribcage, its rapid rhythm echoing my internal chaos.

My parents are my initial focus. They're loving, supportive — the kind of parents many wish for. But how would they react to this truth? I can imagine their surprise, their baffled faces. I can almost see my mom's worried look, my dad's furrowed brow. Would they understand? Would they accept me?

I rehearse the scene in my head. "Mom, Dad, I'm gay." The words are simple but hold an earth-shaking weight, a deep significance. They're the keys to a door I've had locked for too long. They mark a path to a world where hiding and pretending aren't the norms.

But what happens next? After the initial shock, the confusion? Would our relationships change? Would they see me differently, treat me differently? The very thought sends a wave of nausea through me.

Then, there are my classmates — the people I see every day. Those who think they know me, who have their own ideas of who Ethan is. I'm already the odd one out, the butt of hushed jokes and hidden smirks. Coming out would only emphasise my difference, magnify the spotlight on me.

But I ponder, maybe it could also breed understanding. Maybe it would give them a peek into the real me. Maybe it could help me find allies — friends who take me as I am.

Coming out. It's a voyage, a shift. It's about self-acceptance, about being honest with myself and the world around me. It's about stepping out from behind the shadows, about letting go of the fear that's kept me shackled.

But it also includes risks. It means vulnerability, exposing myself to possible pain and rejection. It's a leap of faith, a step towards a future as uncertain as it is hopeful.

As I sit here, on the edge of my bed, fear and anticipation wrestling within me, I realise something. Coming out isn't just about the revelation, the admission. It's not only about the reactions, the consequences.

It's about me. It's about accepting who I am, embracing my identity. It's about breaking the chains of fear and stepping into the light, into a world where I can be myself.

And despite all the anxiety, all the unknowns, I find that I am ready. I am equipped to face whatever comes, ready to accept my truth. Because no matter what, I'm still Ethan. I'm still me. And I am proud of that.

⁂

As the sun begins to wink over the horizon, its first rays streaking the sky with bands of orange and pink, my mom's soft knock reverberates through my bedroom door.

"Ethan, you're going to be late for school," she alerts, her voice laced with the kind of gentle warmth that never fails to envelop me like a cozy blanket.

I had been deep in thought, my mind navigating the tumultuous ocean of feelings and revelations that had swamped me in the wake of my introspection. Lifting my eyes from my tucked-in position on the bed, I call out, "I'm not feeling well, Mom. I think I'm going to stay home today."

There's a moment of silence, then the soft click of the door handle turning. She steps inside, her expression etched with worry. "Are you okay, honey?" she asks, her eyes skimming over me as if searching for visible signs of illness.

I nod, offering her a small smile. "Just need some rest, Mom."

The worry is visible in her eyes, the questions she's holding back. Yet, she doesn't push. Instead, she comes closer, her cool hand briefly on my forehead, before she nods. "Alright, Ethan. Holler if you need anything, alright?"

Once she's gone, the door shut softly behind her, I pull my laptop towards me. The screen's blue-white glow in the soft morning light feels like my personal guiding light, a lighthouse guiding me through the stormy seas of uncertainty and fear.

Finding answers on the internet provides a weird kind of comfort. I'm not the pioneer on this journey, nor will I be the last. There are countless others who've found themselves in the same boat, dealing with the same concerns, the same doubts.

There are endless stories—tales of acceptance and rejection, of joy and heartache. But beneath them all, a shared thread runs—the thread of courage, of authenticity, of staying true to oneself.

As I sift through these shared experiences, I sense a feeling of solidarity, a sense of connection. It's reassuring, reminding me I'm not solo in this fight. There are others out there who understand, who have faced similar challenges and come out stronger.

There's this story about a guy named Julian who got disowned by his family after coming out. Another one about a girl, Lucy, who found acceptance and support from her loved ones. And a story about a transgender teen, Max, who faced prejudice and bullying but found acceptance and love in the most unexpected places.

Every story is distinct, each journey different. But they all arrive at the same end—self-acceptance, self-love, self-identity.

As I dive further into this online chest of shared experiences, I stumble upon a forum dedicated to helping people come out to their loved ones. There are suggestions, tips, and more importantly, reminders that everyone's journey is unique, as are the responses they'll get.

One post underlines the importance of patience. "Remember," it reads, "coming out is a process, not an event. It can take time for people to understand and adjust to what you are telling them. It might be as new and shocking for them as it was for you when you first acknowledged your feelings."

I pen that down in my notes, underscoring the term 'process.' It resonates. I recall the turmoil that roiled within me when I first began to grapple with my emotions—the bewilderment, the denial. It'd be unjust to demand instant acceptance when it took me time to make peace with my own identity.

Another post encourages choosing a secure and comforting setting for the conversation. "Once you've decided to tell them," it counsels, "pick an environment where you feel at ease and secure. And keep in mind, it's not about the ideal moment, but the apt moment."

This prompts reflection. Is there ever an apt moment for such revelations? As I delve deeper into the post, I grasp the message it intends to deliver. The apt moment is less about precise timing and more about readiness—when I am poised to disclose, when I am fortified enough to confront any response, be it positive or negative.

Yet another entry discusses preparing for a spectrum of reactions. "Everyone reacts differently. Some might be accepting, some confused, some may react negatively. But remember, their first reaction may not be their last. People often need time to process the news. And yes, there's still a long way before there won't be such a thing as coming out but, right now, we're still living in this reality."

This insight gives me pause. I realise that I'd steeled myself for instant acceptance or immediate rejection, not contemplating the vast array of responses that could reside in between.

Perhaps the most impactful post I stumble upon goes like this: "Coming out is about you and your truth. You're not responsible for others' reactions or feelings. It's important that you're true to yourself. Your honesty might encourage others to be honest about who they are as well."

This strikes a chord. Amidst my fears and worries, I had lost sight of the most critical aspect. This was about me. It was about being true to myself, living my truth, acknowledging my identity. It was not my responsibility to manage others' feelings or reactions. I could only control my actions, my honesty, and my acceptance of myself.

These stories infuse me with a sense of hope, a sense of understanding. I can see my own fears reflected in their words, my own doubts echoed in their experiences. But I can also see their strength, their resilience, their courage.

And as I sit here, bathed in the light of my laptop screen, immersed in the stories of others who have walked this path before me, I feel a sense of calm descend upon me. I feel a sense of acceptance, of understanding and that I am not alone. I am part of a community, part of a shared experience that transcends age, race, and geography.

This moment feels like a turning point, a milestone on my journey of self-discovery. It's a reminder that my fears, my worries, my doubts, they're valid, they're real. But they're not insuperable. They're not the end of my story. They're merely a part of it.

I close my laptop, a newfound determination pulsating

through me. Yes, the path ahead will be challenging, perhaps terrifying, but it's a path I need to tread. For myself, for my truth, for my freedom. I've lived in the shadows for too long, cloaking myself in fear and uncertainty. But not anymore. It's time to step into the light, to embrace my truth, to live openly and without fear.

※

With a cookie held loosely in one hand and the television remote in the other, I sink into the familiar plush of our well-loved couch. The quiet hum of the television acts as a gentle backdrop, washing over me like soothing white noise. Mom sits beside me, her attention wholly fixed on the screen. Her presence, as always, is warm and reassuring—a constant in my life.

Suddenly, a commercial for a school flashes onto the screen, presenting images of cheerful students, engaging teachers, and bustling classrooms. As I watch, my mind starts to wander, creating a parallel reality far removed from the staged, idealistic one depicted on the screen.

In my daydream, I am entering school amidst the typical hustle and bustle. The hallways echo with the usual symphony of gossiping students, hurrying athletes, and last-minute cramming study groups. Only this time, there is a striking difference: I'm free from the gnawing fear that typically roots itself in the pit of my stomach. There are no hushed whispers echoing behind me, no uncomfortably lingering glances searing into my back. Instead, I'm met with acceptance.

In this vision, I see myself confidently striding down the corridor, an aura of buoyancy replacing my usual hunched posture. Classmates no longer avert their eyes or whisper behind their hands when I pass. Instead, they acknowledge me with casual nods, friendly smiles, and nonchalant 'hey Ethan.' I respond in kind, the familiar knot of anxiety in my chest gradually loosening with each passing interaction.

In this daydream, I'm not the outcast, the misfit to be shunned or ridiculed. I'm simply Ethan — a friend, a classmate, an integral part of the community.

In the classroom, I envision myself confidently raising my hand to answer a question, my voice resonating clearly and steadily. My answers aren't met with stifled giggles or pitiful glances but with nods of agreement. An inner warmth blossoms with each affirmation. I'm no longer the butt of jokes or a figure of pity. I'm just another student, navigating the challenges of high school, learning and growing like everyone else.

The scene shifts to the cafeteria, a large, echoing space filled with the cacophony of clattering trays, animated chatter, and hearty laughter. This time, the sounds aren't daunting or overwhelming, but are rather the harmonious soundtrack to my acceptance.

There, amidst the pulsating energy of teenage life, I sit amongst friends. Our table is a vibrant hub of light-hearted banter, inside jokes, and shared dreams. Our differences are not merely tolerated, but celebrated; our individualities respected. They're privy to my truth, and it doesn't alter their perception of me. To them, I'm simply Ethan—their friend, their confidant.

A wave of yearning washes over me as this vision unfolds. It's not an unreasonable desire, is it? To be accepted as I am, to live my truth openly, without the dread of mockery or rejection.

Just as I'm about to sink deeper into my reverie, a gentle nudge from Mom draws me back to reality. She hands me another cookie, her face illuminated with a soft smile, eyes brimming with warmth. Unaware of my internal musings, she diverts her attention back to the TV, yet her simple gesture—

a comforting offering of sustenance—echoes my deep-seated longing.

I glance at her, then back at the TV, and finally, down at the cookie in my hand. Its simplicity mirrors my wish—not extravagant or outrageous, but grounded in the basic human need for acceptance and love.

The television now showcases a victorious football team from the school, their faces lit with pure joy, camaraderie, and acceptance. I alternate my gaze between the jubilant scene on the screen and my mother's comforting presence, a newfound resolve solidifying within me.

Perhaps my imagined school scenario isn't as fanciful as it seems. Maybe acceptance isn't a far-off dream but a potential reality, a goal worth striving for. With that thought propelling me forward, I bite into the cookie, its sweetness spreading across my tongue, symbolising the hopeful anticipation now fluttering in my heart.

THE WHITE NOISE OF WATER GUSHING FROM THE TAP contrasts sharply with the bathroom's quiet stillness, forming the background score to my thoughts. As I rinse my hands, the cool water cascades over them, leaving a trail of goose-bumps in its wake. Gradually, I raise my gaze to meet my own reflection in the mirror.

In it, I don't see a stranger or an alien entity within my body. Instead, the eyes looking back at me are familiar, their weariness tinged with an indomitable spirit. The reflection is of a boy who has undergone a journey of self-discovery and acceptance, a journey that has brought him face to face with an undeniable truth.

A truth that's echoed in every heartbeat, every breath I've taken since the realisation that I'm gay.

This isn't a bolt from the blue or a sudden revelation, but an affirmation, an acceptance that rings truer each day. It is a truth that's not just accepted but embraced wholeheartedly. A missing piece of my puzzle that has now found its rightful place, painting a complete, unapologetic picture of who I truly am.

Looking at my reflection once more, I notice a spark in my eyes, my shoulders feel a tad lighter. I'm still Ethan, but I'm a new Ethan—an Ethan who's ready to confront himself, to acknowledge his truth, and to live it unabashedly.

A change is in order, a physical manifestation of the emotional and mental transformation occurring within me. The shaggy hair that perpetually obscures my eyes, serving as a barrier between me and the world, needs a trim. I need a style that exudes tidiness, openness, and confidence—attributes of the Ethan I aspire to be.

And my wardrobe—it's time to bid farewell to the oversized, nondescript clothes that allow me to blend into the crowd. I yearn for colours, patterns, styles that speak of personality and individuality. Clothes that reflect the true me, not the version I've fabricated for the world.

I know just the person to help me on this transformative journey—Alex. His unflinching confidence, his unapologetic authenticity, his keen fashion sense—everything about him resonates with the person I'm evolving into.

Tomorrow, I will skip school and visit him. I will share my epiphany, and I will seek his guidance on this transformative journey. It's a step outside my comfort zone, a daunting prospect, but a step I am ready to take. For it's not just about accepting who I am; it's about showcasing who I am to the world, with pride and without fear.

As I shut off the tap, the torrent of water dwindling to a drip, a new soundtrack replaces it—the steady, rhythmic beat of my heart, thumping with determination, excitement, and anticipation. I'm ready to step into the world as the authentic Ethan—the Ethan who's confident, accepted, and who loves himself.

A new mirror, a renewed Ethan. And it all begins in this moment.

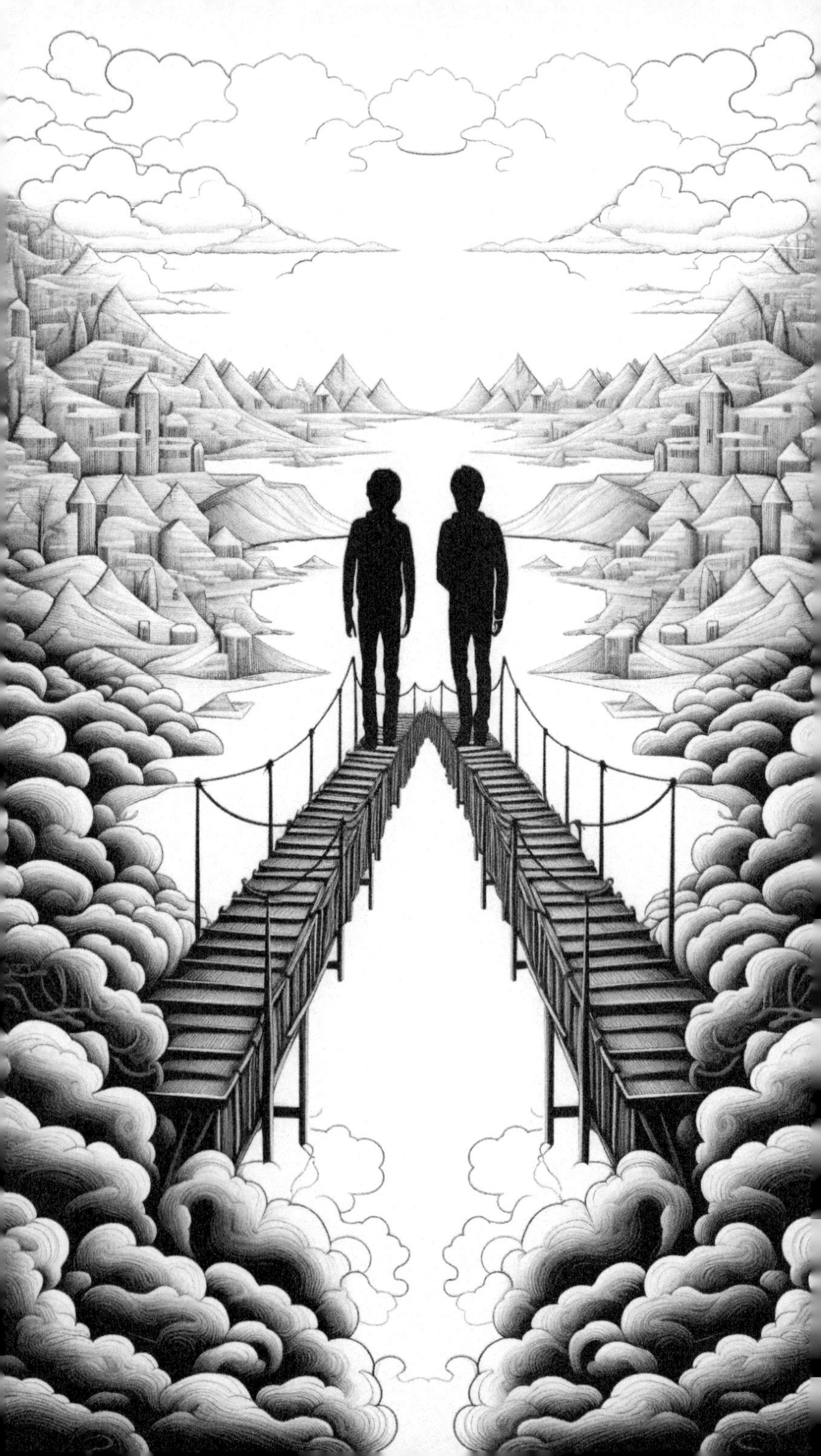

❧ 7 ❧
BUILDING BRIDGES

The morning sun greets me with its tender warmth, as it casts a gentle light through the window that dances off the residual dew on the grass. It's a breathtaking day, too lovely to waste within the confines of a school building. As I pull up to the familiar facade of the hospital, a tempest of butterflies stirs within my stomach. The hospital, which once seemed daunting, now feels comforting, a beacon of familiarity. I draw a deep breath, gathering courage from the crisp morning air, and push open the imposing doors.

The sterile, white corridors of the hospital echo a particular stillness, a calm that reflects my own emotions. This place no longer instills fear and dread. Instead, it's become a haven, a sanctuary where I found acceptance and understanding, and at the core of this sanctuary is Alex.

With each step I take towards his room, the familiarity of the route is etched in my memory. The door creaks softly as I open it, revealing the well-known figure bundled up in bed, his face hidden behind a book.

"Hey, Alex," I greet him, my voice just above a whisper, betraying the unease simmering within me.

His head lifts abruptly at the sound of my voice, surprise flooding his features momentarily before a warm, welcoming smile replaces it. "Ethan! What are you doing here?"

Venturing further into the room, I seat myself on the edge of his bed. "Skipped school," I confess, a sheepish grin tugging at the corners of my lips. "Felt like seeing a friend."

His smile broadens, his eyes twinkling with amusement. "Embracing your rebellious teenage side, are we?"

I shrug, a playful smirk curving my lips. "Possibly."

Our conversation eases into familiar banter, the well-worn rhythm soothing the storm of nerves that had been brewing. Yet, beneath the light-hearted exchanges, a thread of tension weaves its way into our interaction. I'm here with a purpose - a purpose that's been weighing heavily on my heart.

"Ethan," Alex interrupts my internal dialogue, his tone soft yet laced with concern. "There's something else you're here for, isn't there?"

Busted. I offer him a rueful smile. "Is it that so obvious?"

He nods, his eyes brimming with understanding. "To me, it is."

Taking a deep breath, I plunge into my revelation. My words stumble over each other in their eagerness to be voiced. I bare my soul to him, my acceptance of my sexuality, my longing to transform myself, my hope that he will help guide me on this journey.

When I finish, silence stretches out between us. Yet, it isn't an awkward silence; it's filled with understanding and unspoken sentiments.

"Ethan," Alex begins after a moment, his voice gentle yet resolute. "You're filling my heart with pride. Accepting yourself requires courage, and striving to change for the better even more so. I'm honoured that you comfortable in letting me be part of this."

His sincere and genuine words warm my heart, filling it with gratitude. This is why I'm drawn to Alex - his ability to understand, to empathise, to make me feel at home.

In that moment, I comprehend the depth of my feelings for Alex. They go beyond the realm of friendship. They're romantic, affectionate, intense. The butterflies in my stomach stir into motion again, their frantic fluttering matching the tempo of my racing heart.

"Alright," I start, my voice mirroring the uncertainty simmering in my heart. "How do we go about this, Alex? It's not like you're in a condition to simply waltz out of the hospital."

Alex responds with a casual shrug, his eyes twinkling with a hint of playful mischief. "Who's talking about waltzing? I could sashay my way out, if that's easier."

Despite the swarm of concerns in my mind, I find myself laughing at his light-hearted jest. "You're not taking this seriously, are you?"

"I am, Ethan," he retorts, his tone abruptly solemn. "But I also don't want this disease to dominate every aspect of my life. Yes, it's a risk, but it's one I'm willing to take. And for what it's worth, I've been feeling better lately, thanks to the latest treatments."

His words provide some comfort, yet they don't entirely dispel my concerns. "But what about the doctors? The nurses? They'll notice, won't they?"

Alex merely grins, a look of pure mischief painting his face. "I've been here long enough to know their routines, their schedules. Besides, they understand I need to have a life beyond these walls. We're just... bending the rules a little."

"But-" I start, only to be interrupted by Alex's reassuring smile.

"Ethan, trust me," he interjects, his hand reaching out to squeeze mine comfortingly. "We'll manage. You have the plan, I have the timing. Together, we can pull this off."

His confidence is contagious, and despite my anxieties, I find myself getting caught up in the exhilaration of the plan. This represents an opportunity to experience something beyond the stifling boundaries of the hospital and school, a chance to be truly ourselves. As I look into his hopeful eyes, I see a promise - a day of freedom, acceptance, and new beginnings.

"I trust you, Alex," I finally concede, nodding in agreement. "Let's do this."

His grin broadens as he outlines the plan - an audacious escape worthy of a Hollywood blockbuster. It involves a conveniently timed doctors' meeting, some unaware assistance from a friendly nurse, and a borrowed aka stolen lab coat for disguise. It's ambitious, daring, and absolutely Alex.

"Alright," I eventually agree, a thrill of excitement rising within me. "Let's do this. Let's set the town ablaze, metaphorically, of course."

His laughter rings out, filling the room, his eyes gleaming with joy. "That's the spirit, Ethan!"

The gravity of the situation seems to fade under the weight of our shared enthusiasm. We are two teenagers on the verge of an adventure, a rare chance to set aside our worries and just live. Despite his illness, Alex radiates life, his vivacity infectious.

"Yes," I muse, as we laugh and plan, "this is how it's supposed to be."

Tomorrow will be a day of rebellion, transformation, a blossoming of our true selves. But above all, it's a day to be spent with Alex. As I look at him, I comprehend how our lives are interlaced, a tapestry of shared experiences and mutual understanding. And tomorrow, we are about to weave a vibrant new thread into this tapestry.

***

THE MORNING SUN IS BARELY A HINT ON THE HORIZON when my phone buzzes with a message from Alex. The time has come.

> D-Day, Ethan *o*
>
> Are you ready?

> Hahah
>
> Not really...
>
> A little scared of things going south tbh

> Hm
>
> What is a good action movie without some drama? :P

> XD

I respond with a smile on my face and steeling myself for what lies ahead. My heart feels like a live wire in my chest, throbbing with a mix of anxiety and anticipation.

In the quietude of the early morning, with the hospital caught in the tranquil lull before the bustling day begins, Alex and I ready ourselves for our audacious escape. My heart thuds in my chest, each beat amplifying the blend of anticipation and apprehension pulsing through my veins.

"We've got this," Alex assures me, his eyes sparkling with an invigorating mixture of excitement and determination. He glances at me, the corners of his mouth curving upwards into a supportive smile. Despite the seriousness of our upcoming endeavour, I find myself mirroring his grin.

Our plan relies on exact timing and a fair bit of luck. As Alex predicted, a doctors' meeting is scheduled for this morning, a period when the majority of the staff would be occupied for a few minutes. The corridors, typically brimming with activity, are eerily silent and virtually deserted, granting us the perfect opportunity to slip away undetected.

Adorned in a—borrowed—lab coat that's a bit too large, Alex seems oddly fitting in the role of a doctor. He sports a pair of oversized glasses, a whimsical touch intended to complete his disguise. Meanwhile, I choose the less conspicuous guise of a visitor, a role that's easier to maintain.

Our audacious escape plan has nothing to do with a reckless pursuit of thrill or adrenaline, but everything to do with the necessity for a taste of normalcy, a slice of life that doesn't revolve around schedules of medications, therapies, and check-ups. Alex, despite his charm and affability, is confined within these walls by medical decree rather than choice. He could no doubt request a day off, but such is the rigid framework of hospital protocols that a sanctioned outing is near to impossible.

Furthermore, the reality is that we're not merely patients, but boys yearning for a stolen day under the vast open sky, free from the oppressive sterility of a hospital ward. Our plan may be audacious, indeed bordering on reckless, but it springs from an inherent longing for freedom.

The picture in my mind is vivid and tempting: Alex basking under the sun instead of artificial fluorescent lights, a smile on his face as he breathes in the open air, free from the ever-present antiseptic smell. I imagine laughter, exploration, shared moments that aren't confined to a hospital room. A day filled with vibrant hues of life, a stark contrast to the sterile white surroundings we're so accustomed to.

But the thought of this adventure is also shadowed by concern, worry tugging at the edges of my excitement. What if Alex's health deteriorates? What if he needs immediate medical attention and we're not close enough to the hospital? The fear is palpable, a sour taste in my mouth. The consequences of our actions could be grave, potentially worsening Alex's condition.

Despite my worries, I see a spark in Alex's eyes. It's not just the thrill of a clandestine plan—it's the promise of freedom, the prospect of being just a teenager for a day, not a patient. His determination is infectious, drawing me into this daring endeavour despite the risks.

But the risks aren't just about our plan being discovered prematurely, thwarting our escape. There's the possibility of stricter supervision for Alex, of the medical staff's disappointment, of the privileges Alex has earned being revoked. The consequences weigh heavily on me, yet the vision of a day imbued with freedom and normalcy remains too tantalising to resist.

I meet Alex's gaze, seeing in his eyes the unspoken agreement. We both understand the risks, the immense stakes of our audacious plan. Yet the shared determination between us, the silent resolve, empowers us to pursue this day of escape—a day that's genuinely ours.

OUR FIRST OBSTACLE INVOLVES NAVIGATING THE MAZE-LIKE hospital corridors. We've committed the route to memory, meticulously reviewing the hospital floor plans Alex had procured. With our hearts pounding like tribal drums, we initiate our journey, merging into the sparse early morning crowd, our movements subtly disguised by necessity.

Every step, every hushed whisper exchanged, is like

kindling to the fire of adrenaline raging in my veins. My heart echoes the intensity, pulsating against my ribcage like a trapped bird desperate for release. Tension thick as fog envelops us, a tangible entity that mirrors our shared anticipation and apprehension. It clings to us, binding us together as we navigate the intricate web of hospital hallways.

The carpet beneath our feet, an expanse of uninspired monotone, muffles our hurried steps. It's a silent ally in our daring escapade, swallowing the evidence of our passage, each footfall a secret it vows to keep.

We manoeuvre past the nurses' station, our heads lowered, eyes averted. Our hope rests in the early shift nurses being too immersed in the handover process to pay heed to two seemingly innocuous figures passing by.

Suddenly, the shrill squeak of a wheel slices through the early morning tranquility. A gurney, bereft of its usual occupant, is manoeuvred down the hallway by an oblivious orderly. Our breaths hitch in unison, the unexpected sound a sharp reminder of our vulnerability. The moment passes, and we exchange relieved glances, our secret remaining safe.

The thought of them ending the ongoing meeting is like a ghostly lullaby, a reminder of the audacity of our plan. The nebulous hum of authoritative voices, discussing matters far removed from our current undertaking, underscores our rebellion against the confines of hospital routine.

We are spectres, threading through a fluorescent-lit purgatory, a realm of sterilised smells and sanitised surfaces. Each hallway we traverse is a gauntlet of unseen threats, each corner turned a small triumph on our path to freedom. With each passing second, our fear gradually recedes, replaced by a sense of bold determination, a mutual understanding that our resolve is stronger than any obstacle we might encounter.

Approaching the hospital's main entrance, my nerves threaten to unravel our plot. The reception desk is staffed by a stern-looking woman, her gaze frequently sweeping over the CCTV screens. The realisation that a single well-timed glance could expose us spikes fear in my heart.

Just as we're about to cross our proverbial Rubicon, a resounding crash echoes from a nearby hallway, followed by frantic apologies. The receptionist, startled, diverts her attention towards the commotion. That's our cue. Alex gives my hand a comforting squeeze, and we seize the moment.

Stepping into the outdoors, the crisp morning air hits us like a wave, sweeping away the oppressive tension of the previous hour. Our escape has been successful. We burst into euphoric laughter, the exhilaration of our newfound freedom intoxicating us.

"Can you believe we just did that?" Alex exclaims, his face radiant with victory and exhilaration.

"No," I confess, my laughter fading into a broad grin, "But I'm happy we did."

We pause for a moment, revealing in the reality of our adventure, our mutual act of defiance. The hospital, the embodiment of our constraints, looms behind us, oblivious to the loss of two free spirits it once held.

As we amble away, arm in arm, the morning sunlight casting elongated shadows in front of us, I'm filled with an overwhelming sense of camaraderie and delight. We're no longer just two hospital fella. We are Ethan and Alex, explorers on a mission, joint narrators of a story that is distinctly ours.

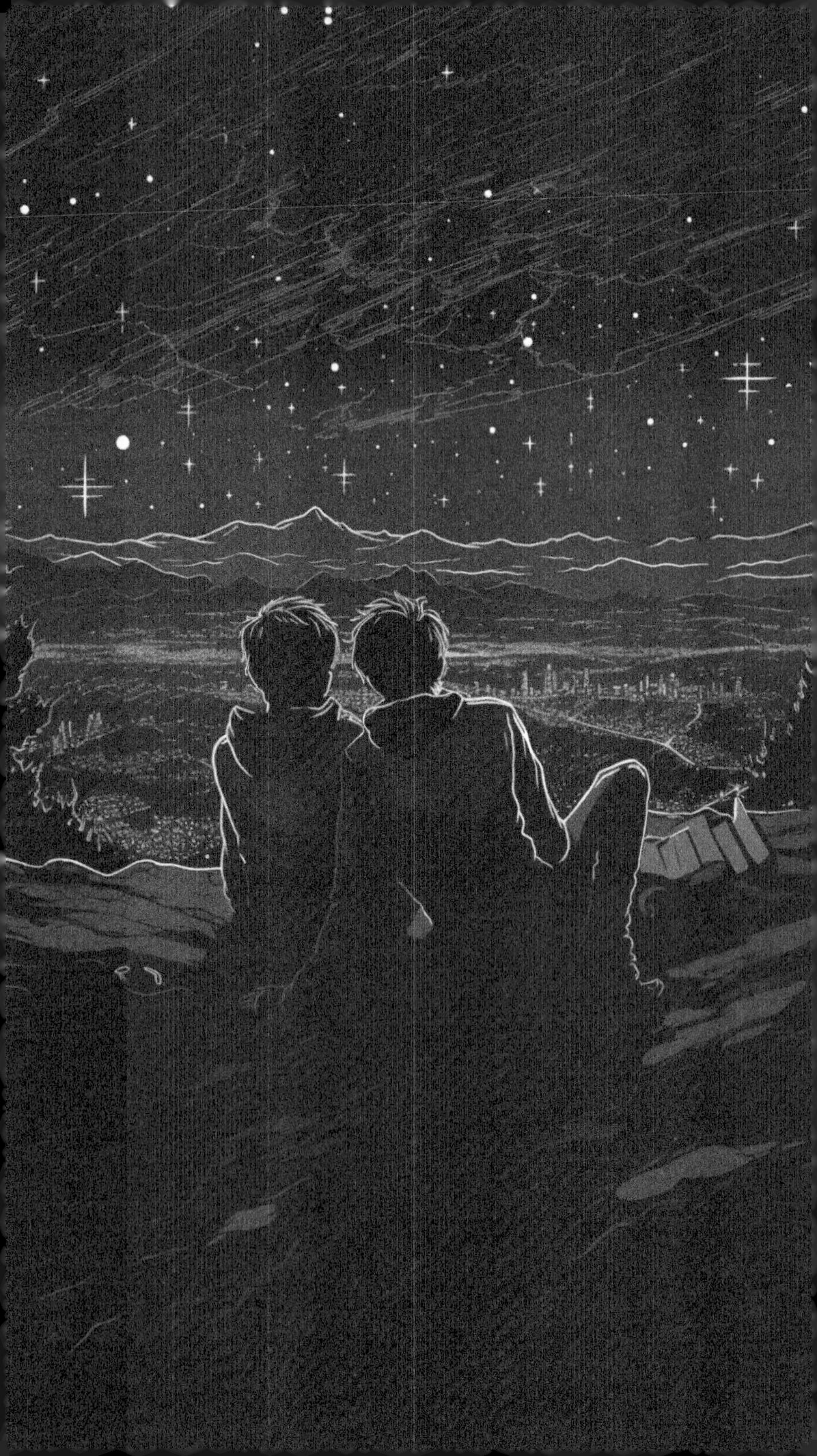

✼ 8 ✼
STARGAZING

The pulsating cityscape blurs past us as we settle into the backseat of the cab. Our hearts drum with the exhilaration of our daring escape, the morning air filled with our shared laughter and anticipation. As we make our way to the shopping mall, the world outside appears more vibrant, offering enticing promises of fresh starts and transformations.

The barbershop, nestled on the first floor of the mall, thrums with activity. Patrons fill the waiting area, their eyes either engrossed in magazines or glued to the large screen airing a football game. Alex and I exchange glances before we approach the reception, our names promptly added to the waiting list.

While waiting, a hefty book sprawled on a glass coffee table grabs our attention. Its glossy pages teem with an array of hairstyles, from pompadours to undercuts, serving as an homage to the artistry of hairstyling. Together, we leaf through it, our fingers brushing over the sleek pages, deliberating which style would best suit me.

"I'll do a French Crop," Alex declares, his finger tracing

the outline of a model flaunting the mentioned hairstyle, "And for you...a Long Fringe and Mid Fade." He gestures to another image, his eyes alight with mischief.

I gaze at the image, a fleeting wave of apprehension washing over my face. "Are you sure? It's...different."

"Exactly!" Alex exclaims, his face breaking into a wide grin. "Today is about change, Ethan. About embracing our true selves. What better way to symbolise that than a new hairstyle?"

His words reverberate in the air, striking a profound note amidst the casual chatter of the barbershop. I find myself nodding, my heart resonating with anticipation.

As we wait, we engage in an easy conversation. We discuss everything and nothing in particular, our words intertwining into a delicate tapestry of companionship and shared experiences. We reminisce about our escape, our laughter filling the room, attracting intrigued looks from the other customers.

When our names are finally announced, we rise and approach the barber's chair. I observe as the barber begins working on Alex, the drone of the trimmer merging with the soothing background music of the shop. Alex's eyes meet mine in the mirror, his expression relaxed, a contagious smile on his lips. A wave of contentment washes over me, realising that for the first time in a long while, we are genuinely happy.

With Alex's transformation complete, it's my turn. As the barber snips and styles, I find myself deep in thought. This is more than just a new hairstyle. It's a symbol of my emerging acceptance, an affirmation of the person I am evolving into.

When the barber finally swivels my chair around, my heart flutters in my chest. I barely recognise the individual staring back at me. The fresh haircut instills in me a renewed sense of confidence, a recognition of the internal transformation. And then I catch sight of Alex, his face reflecting my astonishment and admiration.

Emerging from the barbershop, a surge of elation sweeps over me. A fresh look, a shifted perspective, and the unwavering support of Alex have instilled in me a sense of pride and self-confidence I've never before experienced. As we start strolling, I catch Alex sneaking lingering glances my way. His eyes carry a sparkle I've never noticed before, and the corners of his lips tilt upward in a genuine smile.

"What?" I chuckle, glancing at him. "Do I have a stray hair on my face?"

Alex halts mid-step, his smile broadening, but his gaze remains intense and serious. His hand lifts, gingerly brushing a stray lock of hair from my face. The contact sends a jolt of excitement coursing through my veins, a sensation so uniquely stirring and intoxicating.

"No, Ethan..." He begins, his voice deep and resonant, "You just...you look beautiful. You are beautiful."

I stand there, my mind grappling to comprehend his words. Beautiful? Me? The world around me seems to slow, the bustling noise of the mall gradually receding into the background. My heart thumps in my chest, the significance of his words sinking in. The trace of his touch lingers on my skin, a gentle phantom caress.

Alex has witnessed me at my lowest and my highest. He's been there when I was shattered and scarred, and now, when I stand tall, embracing who I am. His words aren't hollow flattery. They are candid, heartfelt, reflecting the depth of our shared journey.

But what does this imply for us? For our friendship? And how do I feel about it? Before I can delve further, the silence is shattered by the comically loud rumble of Alex's stomach. He chuckles, punctuating our intense exchange with a sheepish grin.

"I don't know about you, but I could eat a horse," he quips, shifting the subject and restoring our typical banter.

We enjoy brunch at a quaint café in the mall, with Alex entertaining me with tales of his audacious exploits in the hospital. But even as we laugh and feast, my mind repeatedly drifts back to the moment outside the barbershop.

The delicate touch on my face, the fervour in his eyes, the sincerity in his voice – all are indelibly etched into my memory. I can still sense the heat of his hand, still hear the soft cadence of his voice. I find myself revisiting the moment again and again, each replay ushering in a flood of emotions – surprise, confusion, joy, and something else. Something new and profound that I can't quite identify.

Observing Alex across the table, his laughter reverberating around us, I acknowledge that our relationship has shifted. We're more than just friends now. There's a connection, a pull that's considerably stronger and deeper.

And as I sit here, engrossed in my thoughts, I realise I'm embracing the change. I'm prepared to navigate this new dynamic, ready to let it unravel. The day is all about accepting change, isn't it? And if this is part of it, I'm more than willing to embrace it.

We emerge from the shopping mall, arms loaded with bags of new clothes and accessories, our laughter echoing in the air. Stepping out, we find the sun poised low in the sky, casting a warm golden luminescence over the city. A playful glint flickers in Alex's eyes as he flags down a taxi and hops in without uttering a word.

"Alex, where are we heading?" I inquire as the cab darts through the cityscape.

"Trust me," is his only response, the grin never wavering from his face.

The taxi veers away from the urban bustle, beginning a

winding climb up a nearby mountain. It comes to a halt at a deserted viewpoint overlooking the sprawling city. Stepping out, I find myself stunned by the panoramic vista. The city sprawls out beneath us, bathed in the glow of the setting sun, with buildings casting long shadows across the landscape.

"Alex, how did I not know about this place?" I ask him, my eyes wide with wonder.

A mysterious smile dances on his lips, filled with secrets as ancient as time. As he gazes upon the distant cityscape, his voice is tinged with nostalgia. "When I was a kid, my parents would bring me here. It was... it still is my sanctuary. In the middle of life's noise pollution, this place... it's a symphony of silence. It's a reminder that even the busiest beings need a moment of tranquility."

We recline on the soft grass, nature's carpet cradling us. The sinking sun plays the role of a master painter, filling the canvas of the sky with hues of orange and red, each shade a testament to an artist's dream. The whispering wind, the rustling leaves, all bear witness to our shared solitude.

As day yields to twilight, Alex, his face reflecting the ethereal beauty above, turns towards me. His voice is softer than the murmuring breeze, his words crafting a melody that resonates in the deepest corners of my heart.

"Do you ever look at the stars, Ethan?" His question is so unexpected that I can't suppress a chuckle.

"Stars? Now? Have you gone star crazy, Alex?"

His laughter rings out alongside mine before he gestures towards the infinite expanse above, where the twilight sky is now adorned with the first sparkling jewels of the night. "No, silly. Just look at them. They are remnants of past eons, bearers of cosmic histories, unique and alone. Yet, despite their solitary existence, they are part of a stunning constellation. They are... together."

His words, unassuming yet impactful, swirl around us,

crafting a picture of such profound beauty it steals my breath away. I turn to him, his figure bathed in the soft glow of the fading day, his features a study in divine elegance.

"I...Alex..."

He silences me with a simple gesture, his eyes, brimming with emotions, holding my gaze. "Ethan, I wish to mirror those stars. To exist in an infinite expanse yet not be alone. To share my existence with someone who comprehends the depth of me. And... I long for that 'someone' to be you."

The sincerity in his voice, the raw honesty of his words, strike a chord in my heart, reverberating in the silent recesses of my mind. He has feelings for me. Alex, the mysterious Alex, harbours feelings for me. His gaze steady, his hand extends towards me as if offering a lifeline.

And before I can fully grasp the magnitude of his confession, he closes the distance between us, his lips brushing gently against mine. A surge of heat erupts within me, warmth radiating from my core. I find myself responding, our rhythms synchronising in a dance as timeless as the universe itself. It's a tender promise, an affirmation of beginnings anew.

As we separate, our breaths commingling in the cooling air, I look into his eyes. The glittering city lights below us shimmer in their depth, creating twinkling stars of our own private cosmos. His hand intertwines with mine, a wordless confirmation of the bond we now share.

In that moment, with the cityscape as our audience, the stars as our companions, a profound realisation settles within me. Like those distant stars, we are no longer solitary entities. We have each other, two souls intertwined in the cosmic ballet of destiny. In the grand design of the universe, we are not alone. We are... together.

Our eyes lock, the descending sun creating a serene backdrop to our silent acknowledgement. The kiss has ignited a spark between us, a flame resilient against the winds of uncertainty. As our lips part, a lingering sensation remains, both foreign yet oddly comforting. Our breaths synchronise, hearts drumming against our chests, composing a sweet symphony audible only to us.

His gaze is the first to deviate, descending to the hand lying between us. He claims it as his own, his fingers tracing my palm as if reading a narrative etched in my skin. Each touch triggers sparks coursing through my veins, gently reaffirming the connection we've shared, the bond now taking shape.

His gaze lifts, reconnecting with mine. In his eyes, I detect a certainty I've not seen before, an expression that carries more than simple affection. It's a look of understanding, of acceptance, a look that unapologetically proclaims 'I see you'.

"Can I...?" he murmurs, his voice barely perceptible against the soft hum of the city beneath us. I comprehend his request, the appeal to explore the burgeoning bond between us, to delve deeper into the intimacy we've just encountered.

I give a nod of assent, my breath catching as his fingers trace the contours of my face. His touch is as light as a feather, imbued with reverence as if he were handling something precious. He traces the line of my jaw, my cheekbones, the curve of my eyebrow, his gaze never straying from mine.

His fingers then trace the outline of my lips, an electrifying touch that leaves me gasping for air. His lips soon supplant his fingers, the heat from his kiss burning through me, consuming me in a tidal wave of raw passion.

His arms weave around me, drawing me closer. I surrender to his embrace, the warmth of his body infiltrating mine. The world beyond us blurs into irrelevance as my attention centres solely on him – the flavour of his kiss, the perfect fit of his body against mine, the assurance that I am seen, comprehended, cherished.

Our bodies move as one, each touch orchestrating a symphony of desire and longing. His hand ventures under my shirt, his fingers fluttering on my skin, sending shivers rippling down my spine. His hips move against mine with a desperation that mirrors my own, a silent entreaty for more.

As our bodies press closer, his hips subtly tilt against mine, the intensity of the contact sending sparks of anticipation through our entwined forms. There is a rawness in this movement, a primal instinct driving us further into a dance of intimacy and desire. I feel every ridge of his body, every hard muscle against my own as our hips align in rhythm, merging our warmth into a singular burning entity.

The heat intensifies as he grinds against me, the friction eliciting a gasp from my lips. Every push, every pull, is met with equal fervour, our bodies engaging in an unspoken dialogue, speaking volumes in the language of desire and longing. A wave of pleasure washes over me, a shuddering breath escaping my lips as his hips rock against mine.

A low groan rumbles from his chest, a sound swallowed by our closeness, resonating within the tight space between us. My fingers clutch at his back, tracing the contours of his body, the muscles tensing and flexing under my touch. His response is a desperate thrust of his hips, our bodies entwining even more intimately in a shared rhythm of passion.

Our boundaries blur, the line where he ends and I begin becoming indistinguishable. It's a dance of intimacy, an exploration of unknown territories that leaves us gasping, craving for more. His movements grow more deliberate, his hips aligning perfectly against mine, our bodies responding in harmony.

Our pulses race, echoing the frantic beat of our shared

rhythm. The air around us is charged with electric tension, each of his thrusts, each grind against my hips serving as a silent plea for more - an insatiable desire that is both intoxicating and overwhelming. It's a dance as old as time, yet it feels new, exciting, a thrilling exploration of our shared intimacy.

We lose ourselves in the kiss, in the exchange of emotions too profound for words. The intimacy of the moment leaves me breathless, a wild rush of exhilaration surging through my veins.

As we draw back, panting and flushed, our foreheads rest against each other. Our eyes meet, the intensity of his gaze setting my heart aflutter. We recline there, the ambient sounds of the city filling the silence that hangs between us.

In his arms, our hearts beating in harmony, I discover a tranquility I've never before known. This is the embodiment of being truly seen, of being truly loved. In his eyes, I find acceptance. In his arms, I find home.

***

DAY HAS GIVEN WAY TO NIGHT, THE CITY LIGHTS twinkling beneath us, echoing the stars overhead. The world continues its rhythm around us, oblivious to the transformative event that has just unfolded atop this mountain. Here, within his arms, I find myself. I find love.

As we recline here, basking in the afterglow of our shared connection, the eerie melody of my ringtone cuts through the air, shattering our blissful moment. With a frown, I retrieve the phone from the depths of my pocket. A flicker of panic ignites in my chest when I identify the caller.

"Mom," I declare, offering Alex an apologetic expression. He merely reciprocates with a nod, sharing a comforting squeeze before distancing himself.

"Hey, Mom," I utter, endeavouring to maintain a steady voice.

"Ethan? Where are you?" Her voice is infused with concern, the frantic edge to it making my heart plummet. "It's getting late, and you're not home yet. Is everything okay?"

"Everything's fine, Mom," I assure her, casting a glance at Alex, who regards me with an understanding look. "I'm with a friend right now."

"Since when do you have friends?" she queries. I can discern the hurt in her tone, the unspoken questions that lurk in the ensuing silence.

"We... we've been friends for some time now, Mom. We met in the hospital" I respond, my gaze shifting back to Alex. "I just... I just didn't mention it."

Before she can reply, I interject. "I'll be home soon, okay? I promise."

"Okay," she murmurs, but I can sense she isn't entirely convinced. "Just... be safe, okay?"

"I will, Mom. I promise."

With that, I terminate the call, fixating on the phone screen for a moment longer before returning it to my pocket. The joyous bubble that enveloped us has burst, replaced by a profound silence we can't seem to dispel.

"I understand," Alex finally breaks the quiet, "Our time is up." His words carry a melancholy that mirrors my own, the harsh reality of our situation hitting us like a physical blow.

"We should..." I initiate, but my voice falters, incapable of completing the sentence. Instead, I lean into him, pressing my lips against his in a bittersweet kiss. It tastes of farewell, a testament to what might have been, a lingering reminder of the intimacy we had shared.

As the taxi arrives, with the hospital casting an ominous shadow in front of us, I pause to gaze at Alex. The dim light of the city street casts a subtle glow on his face, emphasising the softness in his eyes, the gentle curve of his lips.

"Alex," I begin, my voice barely above a whisper. "I...I don't have the words to describe how much this day meant to me."

His hand rises to cradle my cheek, the warmth of his touch anchoring me. His thumb traces the line of my cheekbone, a soft smile playing at his lips. "Neither can I, Ethan," he echoes, his voice imbued with a warmth that sets my heart aflutter. "Neither can I."

And then, beneath the artificial light of the city, we share one final kiss. A kiss that tastes of longing, of trepidation, of hope. A kiss that hints at a future day, a future where we can be true to ourselves, where we can be united.

With that promise lingering in the air, I watch as Alex steps out of the taxi, his figure swallowed by the hospital. As the taxi pulls away, I can't resist glancing back, one thought resonating in my mind:

This isn't a goodbye. It's a beginning.

As soon as the front door gives a creaking surrender, I'm instantly enveloped in a deluge of hallway fluorescent light. My parents occupy the doorway, their apprehensive countenances a stark contrast to their usually calm demeanour. This scene eerily mirrors the last time they confronted me this way, the memory of hospital beds and sustained injuries edging closer to overwhelming me.

"Ethan," my mother's voice trembles, her eyes brimming with concern. "Are you okay?"

"Yes, Mom," I answer, stepping inside and shrugging out of my coat. My father remains silent, his unyielding gaze landing on me like an immense burden. His eyes carry a silent entreaty, an unspoken question he fears to articulate.

"Where were you?" he eventually voices, his deep tones breaking the silence that has descended upon the room.

"I was...I was out with a friend," I reveal, evading their scrutinising gaze. "We lost track of time."

The room is once again filled with silence, the density of their concern and fear threatening to smother me. But they refrain from further questioning. Perhaps they dread the potential answers, or maybe they decide to afford me the space I so direly require.

"I'm going to take a shower," I mumble, attempting to lighten the oppressive atmosphere. My mother offers a nod and a feeble smile, while my father continues to study me, his gaze unwavering.

Once the bathroom door is securely closed behind me, I release a sigh, leaning against the chilly tiles. Water cascades over me, each drop a sharp reminder of the austere reality I've returned to. The image of Alex, his tender smile, and the sensation of his touch persist in my mind, starkly contrasting my current situation. The sanctuary I discovered in his presence now feels like a distant dream.

In the tranquil solitude of the shower, doubts start to insinuate themselves into my thoughts, whispering like demons in my ear. Is this genuinely what I desire? Is risking our friendship worth it? Could I endure losing Alex if things were to go awry?

These questions whirl around me, engulfing my thoughts, my fears augmented by the drumming water. The knot in my stomach tightens, a sharp spike of anxiety surging through me. The terror of rejection, of heartbreak, hangs over me like a menacing shadow, its dark tendrils threatening to extinguish the light Alex had sparked within me.

At last, I switch off the shower, wrapping a towel around my waist. As I exit the bathroom, I can sense the weight of the day sinking into my bones. I need rest. I need clarity.

But as I recline on my bed, staring at the blank ceiling, the doubts surge back, dragging me under their relentless tide. My mind is a maelstrom of thoughts - Alex's face, his words, the dread of losing him all vie for dominance.

Yet amidst the chaos, a beacon of hope flickers, a guiding light in the tempest. The memory of Alex's touch, the warmth of his words, the affection in his eyes. They serve as a salve for my fears, an assurance that perhaps this risk is worthwhile.

As sleep begins to claim me, one certainty crystallises: regardless of what unfolds next, my feelings for Alex are genuine. They form a part of me. And maybe, it's time I accept them, confront my fears, and take a leap of faith.

With that thought lingering in my mind, I yield to the day's exhaustion, hoping that the morrow would bring the courage I need to face whatever lies ahead.

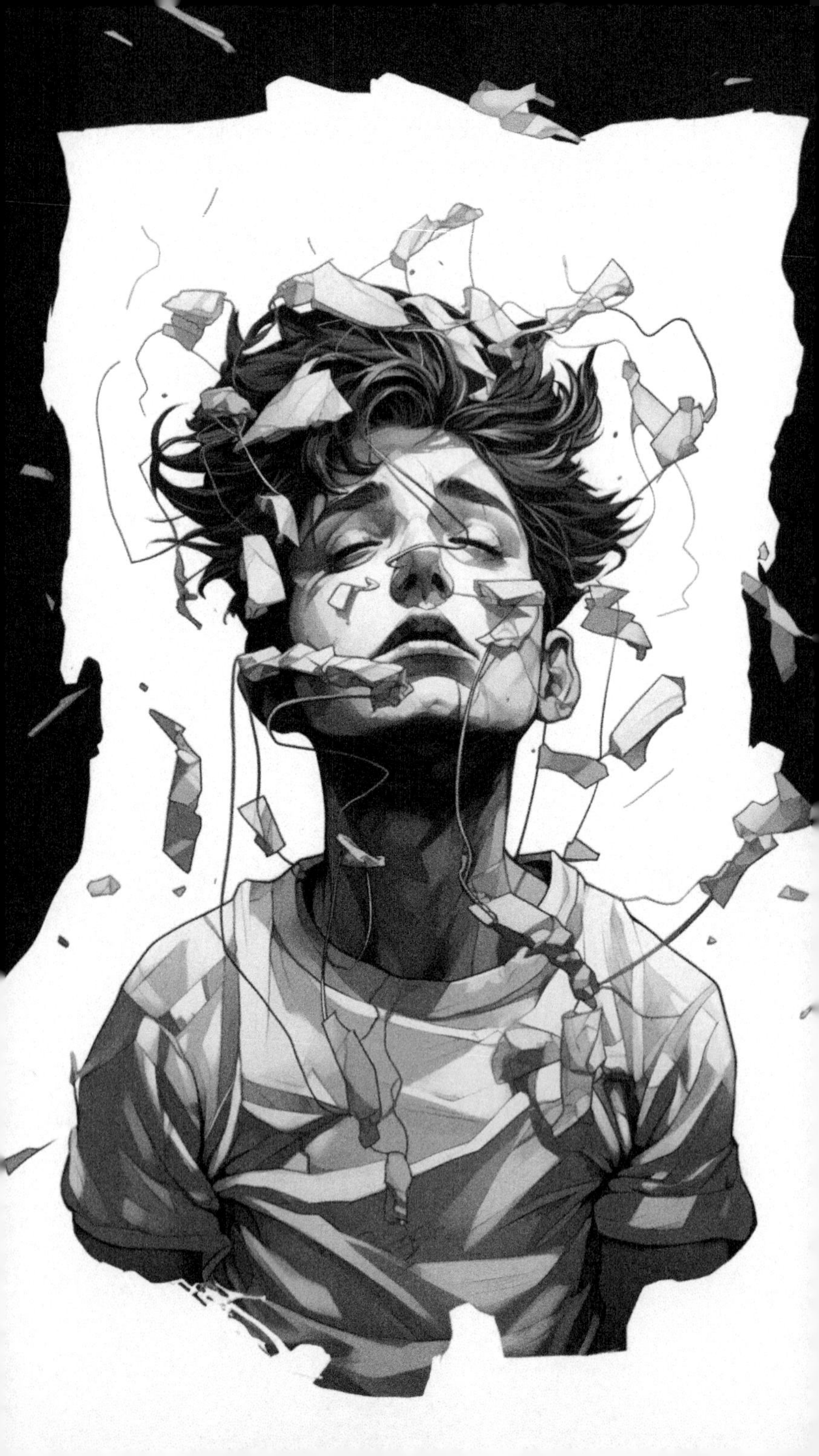

9
THE MASK FALLS

As the dawn unfurls its golden fingers through the blinds, the chirping of birds serves as my natural alarm clock, rousing me to a new day and a newfound sense of resolve. The reflection that gazes back at me from the mirror is no longer a stranger; it's me - Ethan, complete with a new haircut, fresh clothes, and a confident aura radiating from my being. The long fringe accentuates the determination residing in my eyes, while the mid-fade lends an edge, a loud proclamation of my intent not to blend in any longer.

The moment my shoes strike the pavement outside my home, it's as though I've stepped onto a stage; the world is my audience, and I'm prepared to play my part. Each step resonates with this newfound confidence, a sense of self-assuredness that seems to vibrate in the air around me. I'm a new person - no longer in a cocoon trapped in self-doubt and insecurity but a butterfly delighting in the beauty of his transformation.

As I stride into the school grounds, I sense a shift in the atmosphere. Whispers, like invisible currents, flutter around me, filled with curiosity and surprise. The world registers this transformation within me, acknowledging the seismic shift that has occurred deep within my soul. Eyes that would usually skim over me now linger a little longer, surprise and intrigue gleaming within their depths. It's as if I've burst from my cocoon of obscurity, my transformation too dazzling to overlook.

Yet amidst this surge of positivity and newfound self-confidence, I sense an ominous shadow creeping in, eager to engulf my radiant aura. The corridor stretches out before me, seeming to expand with each step, setting the stage for an imminent confrontation. At the corridor's far end, a group of familiar faces sneer, their laughter echoing through the silent hallway, sending shivers down my spine. They are like gathering storm clouds, ready to unleash a torrent of taunts and jeers, eager to extinguish my confident flame.

The pit of my stomach churns, waves of past memories crashing against my conscious mind. Their faces are etched into my nightmares, a constant, painful reminder of my past. But today, as I meet their gaze, the fear in my eyes is replaced by a spark of defiance. They are the dark clouds that have persistently loomed over me, but now, I am ready to face the storm.

"Look at the princess. Got a new haircut, new clothes," Jackson, the principal tormentor, calls out, his voice reverberating through the hallway. The others chime in with laughter, their derisive chuckles a bitter symphony that sends a shiver down my spine. Fear twists my gut as memories of past encounters flash in my mind.

However, today, I'm not the same. The fear persists, but so does my resolve. Meeting Jackson's gaze, I gather my courage and retort, "It's a pity you can't do the same. Stuck in the same, aren't you Jackson? The same dull haircut, the same tired clothes, the same stale jokes. It's truly sad."

The corridor plunges into silence, the echoes of my words lingering in the air. Jackson's face turns crimson, his eyes bulging with surprise and anger. His cronies shift from him to me, visibly disoriented by my unexpected retaliation. The wheels turn in their heads as they grapple with the sudden shift in dynamics.

"And look at you guys, just blindly following Jackson. Can't you think for yourselves? Or is that asking too much?" I continue, my voice steady. They exchange uncertain glances, then look to Jackson, their self-assured smiles replaced by apprehension.

"Don't you dare speak to us like that!" Jackson roars, taking a threatening step towards me. But I stand my ground, the fear no longer holding me captive. "Or what, Jackson? You'll beat me up again? Go ahead. You might bruise me, but you won't break me. Not anymore."

He halts, his face red, fists clenched, "You'll regret this, Ethan," he snarls, his voice barely audible. But I merely shrug, an insolent smile playing on my lips.

"I'm looking forward to it, Jackson," I respond, sidestepping him, leaving him rooted amidst the stunned silence of the corridor.

Each heartbeat thunders in my chest like a drumbeat of war, adrenaline fuelling each pulsation as I walk away. The familiar sensation of dread, a cold gnawing sensation in my stomach, persists. It is the spectre of the past, waiting in anticipation of Jackson's promise of revenge, the possibility of my triumph igniting a desire for retribution within him. Yet, this fear is different from the dread that used to overshadow my every waking moment. It is an echo, softer and quieter than before, a fragment of what used to be.

This fear doesn't weigh me down or shroud my mind in terror. Instead, it serves as a reminder of the courage that has taken root in my heart, a testament to the struggle that has led me to this turning point.

Running through my veins with greater force and more vitality is a sense of triumph that tastes sweeter than any fear could sour. An effervescent joy bubbles within me, ready to spill over. This joy is born from self-realisation and fortitude that had been lurking beneath my exterior, waiting for the right moment to surface. It affirms and validates that yes, I possess the strength, I possess the courage to stand up for myself, to confront my tormentors.

And as I proceed down the corridor, leaving behind the stunned silence and the seething fury of Jackson, a profound truth settles in. I am no longer the same Ethan they once knew. I am no longer the timid, scared boy who would cower under their mockery. I have shed that skin, broken free from the cocoon that kept me hidden and emerged as the person I truly am.

The mask, the disguise I wore for so long has crumbled, shattered into a million pieces under the force of my newfound self-assuredness. What lies beneath isn't the weak and fearful Ethan. No, it's a stronger, braver version of me. One that isn't afraid to accept himself, to express himself, to confront his fears, and to fight for his beliefs.

It's a metamorphosis, a transformation that's been subtle yet powerful. I've discovered my true self. A self that is undeniably, unashamedly, Ethan. And my walk down the corridor is not merely a walk anymore. It's a stride into a new beginning, a stride of self-discovery and acceptance. My fears, doubts, and past do not bind me any longer. I am free, I am brave, and above all, I am me.

Days have trickled by since my spectacular re-entry into the school scene, the atmosphere radiating with my newfound confidence. The mirror reflects a transformed image, a portrait of a person who isn't afraid to stand tall and shine brightly amidst the grey palette of high school life. Yet, a change is palpable in the air, a tremor of impending catastrophe that looms ominously.

I notice the shift in Jackson and his peers' demeanour. Their typically smug expressions are replaced by a hardness, a chilling resolve that raises the hairs on the back of my neck. I spot them huddled in corners, their whispers carried away by the buzz of the school, their sly glances confirming my fears. Something is brewing in their twisted minds, a storm conjured from their resentment and bruised egos.

The more I notice their changed behaviour, the more I remember the Jackson of the past. He was the puppeteer who revelled in pulling at my strings, the tormentor who had made my life a living hell. The memory of him, once faded, starts to sharpen, the edges cutting through my veil of optimism. His threats reverberate in my ears, "You'll regret this, Ethan," words spat out with venomous rage.

I'm unable to shake off the niggling dread that has set up residence in the pit of my stomach. It claws at me, nibbling away at the edges of my newfound confidence. I keep telling myself that I'm no longer the old Ethan, the vulnerable target who'd succumb to their bullying. Yet, I can't deny the prickle of fear crawling under my skin, a silent warning that whispers of the storm Jackson promised.

This gnawing dread is further amplified by the bell that signals the end of the day, a tune that usually brings relief. Today, however, its chime is foreboding. My burgeoning self-confidence, once as sturdy as an asteroid in orbit, now teeters on the brink of a catastrophic plunge.

As the afternoon sunlight streaming through the school's

windows starts to fade, it casts long, monstrous shadows that mirror the gnawing dread inside me. The faces of my peers, typically blurry shapes on the periphery of my existence, sharpen into stark figures of anticipation. Something is coming - a storm brewing in the heart of a school day winding down.

Then, it happens. As quick and unexpected as a summer squall, a hush descends over the crowd, followed by a ripple of laughter. The intercom sparks to life, its loud words an electrifying storm, tearing through the school's tranquillity. Each syllable dropped from a Web Translator's robotic and sterile voice is a lightning bolt, severing the mundane and the routine, making the air crackle with a malicious energy.

"Ethan harbours a secret," the dispassionate, unfeeling voice begins, sowing a toxic seed in the fertile ground of adolescent curiosity. "He's been masquerading among you, hiding behind a glass closet. Now it's time to rip away the mask."

The voice continues, its words drip with an icy precision that makes the bile rise in my throat. The revelation is methodical, surgical, turning my truth into a carnival sideshow. Each statement is a pointed dagger, honed to hurt, humiliate, ostracise.

"And who is the object of his desires?" the voice pauses theatrically, letting the silence swell with dread. "Alex. His new look, his newfound confidence, is nothing more than an attempt to allure another boy."

I feel violated on a raw, guttural level. This is my truth, my secret. They have no right. But the merciless voice presses on, shredding my dignity with every relentless phrase.

"Secret rendezvous, stolen kisses, hushed whispers. A love nurtured in the shadows, away from your prying eyes. But no more."

As if this public revelation isn't diabolical enough, our

phones buzz in unison, taking the cruelty to a new level. It's a multimedia message, sent to everyone — a montage of carefully selected photos of Alex and me, chat snapshots splayed out for all to scrutinise.

In their original context, the photos are innocuous. But the messages, torn from our private conversations, reveal intimate admissions, declarations of affection, interspersed with lies and exaggerations. Stripped of privacy, they transform into damning evidence in this twisted trial conducted by an electronic jury. A burning question lodges itself in my throat: How?! How did they manage to invade the private realm of our phone conversations?

The cacophony of notifications provides a perverse accompaniment to the revealing dialogue playing through the intercom. The mingling sounds form a discordant symphony, the soundtrack to my life spiralling into chaos.

As the final word echoes through the hallways, silence descends, bearing down like a weight. There's no roar of outrage, no shock-induced outburst. Just a lull, the calm before the storm.

Shock and revulsion wash over the crowd. Whispers grow into a hurricane of voices, laughter bouncing off the walls like hyenas feasting on a carcass. The montage of pictures, the messages, the revelation - all turn into a cruel spectacle of voyeurism.

I am no longer Ethan. I am the scandal, the spectacle, the exposed secret. The mask has fallen, and beneath it lies a boy stripped of his dignity, his privacy violated, his love turned into perverse entertainment.

Standing in the epicentre of the storm, I am pelted by their words, pierced by their laughter. I am drowning in a sea of whispers, suffocating under the weight of their stares, my world collapsing around me. The chaos around me mirrors the turmoil within, a cruel reflection of my internal devastation. I am experiencing a cataclysm, a personal apocalypse.

Jackson and his cronies have found a way to out me, to grotesquely expose my sexuality without getting caught. My heartbeat stutters, the blood drains from my face as my worst fear is manifested in the avalanche of whispers and laughs sweeping through the school.

The world spins, a carousel out of control, as those words, the intimate details of my life, are weaponised and fired at me. I can hear my heart pounding in my ears, a chilling symphony accompanying the public spectacle my life has suddenly become.

Chaos reigns as whispers turn into murmurs, murmurs into pointed laughter, and pointed laughter into a full-blown roar. The corridors I'd walked down with newfound confidence seem alien now, filled with judgemental eyes and whispering mouths.

I feel the heat of a thousand stares, each one boring into me, stripping away the armour I recently donned. There's no room for defence or explanation. The tidal wave of shock, horror, and betrayal washes over me, threatening to pull me under.

In the frenzy of noise, everything blurs. Faces contort with surprise, some with malice, some with a hurtful delight. The loud murmurings, the accusatory glares, the stifled laughter... it's all a grotesque painting, each stroke a blow to my heart.

My chest tightens, a vice-like grip around my lungs. I can barely breathe. Tears sting the corners of my eyes, but I blink them back fiercely. I won't let them see me break. I won't give them the satisfaction.

Despite this resolve, I am breaking. A devastating, soul-crushing break. The silence I'd held inside me, the truth about my identity, has shattered into a thousand pieces, each piece echoing in the damning laughter around me.

The asteroid has crashed. The school, my world, is engulfed in the smoke of my humiliation. My worst fear plays out on the most public of stages. My newfound confidence is lost in the wreckage, leaving behind a raw, exposed version of me who has never felt more alone.

The bell rings again, signalling one more time the end of the day. But for me, it marks the end of an era. It's a haunting echo that marks the crash of the asteroid, the fall of my mask, and the public outing of my sexuality. The tone, once the harbinger of freedom, now marks my heartbreak.

A volcanic pressure surges within me, intense and relentless, teetering on the edge of eruption. I'm grappling with an unbearable violation, a severe injustice. Yet, my tormentors have overlooked one crucial factor: every volcano inevitably explodes.

I weave through the crowd, my heart pounding an aggressive war drum in my chest.

Breathing in deeply, I taste the stagnant air of the school corridor. It reeks of fear, intolerance, and narrow-mindedness. However, I realise this is an opportunity to change the narrative, a chance I cannot let slip away.

In the midst of the hushed whispers and judgemental glances, I stride forward. Their echoing laughter has assaulted my heart, leaving behind a throbbing pain. But within me, a storm brews, and my anger and defiance rouse like a phoenix stirring from slumber.

"Today, a revelation has been thrust upon you. A truth that is mine and has been forced out into the light, before its time, against my will." The resonance of my voice reverberates through the hall, each syllable chiming with determination. The atmosphere palpably shifts, curiosity and shock humming with anticipation.

"Yes, it's true. I'm gay. I am drawn to Alex." The ensuing silence seems to stretch into eternity. "But this is not a secret of which I was ever ashamed. It is my truth, my journey to discover and embrace. Today, this journey has been forcibly torn from me, exploited, and exposed as a weapon of humiliation and ridicule."

"Shocking, isn't it? Someone being gay, a boy kissing another boy..." Their wide-eyed stares and sharp intakes of breath bear testament to their surprise. "Unsettling, isn't it? But why? Why does my truth, my identity, shake you so? Why does my existence feel like a threat to you?"

I pause, letting my questions reverberate through the pregnant silence.

"We are always encouraged to take pride in who we are, to celebrate our uniqueness. But the moment we dare to be different in a way that society refuses to accept, we are shamed. We are mocked, even demonised."

"But why should we hide ourselves? Why should we enshroud ourselves in fear and shame? Is it because our love is inferior? Are our feelings are less valid? Is it because our existence is less significant?"

"NO," I press on, my voice resonant, my resolve unwavering. "Our love is not a lesser love. Our feelings are not less valid. Our existence is not less significant. We are not aberrations. We are as real and beautiful as any other."

My heart thunders in my chest, rhythmically underlining my impassioned speech. Each word feels like a punch thrown at bigotry, each sentence an assault against ignorance and intolerance.

"My identity is not fodder for your mockery or a plaything for your amusement. It's as real, as profound, as anyone's. This is my truth. This is me. I will not hide it, not anymore. I won't let it become a source of shame or ridicule.

And I will stand, proud and unashamed, even if I must stand alone."

A surge of adrenaline punctuates my words with an intensity that resonates against the silent walls. I stand tall, the echo of my proclamation a testament to my resilience and acceptance.

"Being gay is not a weakness, it's not a mistake, it's not a sin. It's part of who I am. A part I will no longer hide or deny. So today, I stand before you not as a victim, but as a warrior. A warrior who will fight for his right to love, his right to exist, his right to be acknowledged and accepted."

"I am gay, and I am not ashamed. My love, my identity, can't and won't be diminished by your laughter, your whispers, your intolerance. So mock me, ridicule me, but know this - you cannot break me. Because I am strong, I am proud, and I am valid."

With these words, I observe a flicker of understanding in their eyes - the following silence is not filled with mockery, but rather stunned respect.

In this silence, I am no longer just Ethan, the quiet boy forced out of the closet. I am Ethan, the boy who transformed his darkest fear into a beacon of truth and strength, who rejected shame, who dared to defy.

From the ashes of mockery and humiliation, I rise like a phoenix.

The silence that engulfs me following my proclamation seems to extend into infinity, the air heavy with shock and the gravitas of my words. An ocean of faces, wide-eyed and slack-jawed, stares back at me, a mix of surprise, newfound respect, and lingering disdain. The reactions are as varied as they are profound, mirroring the intricacies of the society we inhabit.

In some faces, I observe the dawning of understanding,

eyebrows furrowing in deep thought as they grapple with my words. Their ignorance has been challenged, their viewpoints adjusted. A handful of others, those nursing similar secrets, appear to regard me with something resembling admiration. Their eyes convey silent gratitude, unspoken applause. Yet, there are those who cling to their smirks, their laughter swallowed, but the derision remaining in their eyes. Their ignorance stands as an impregnable fortress, immune to reason or empathy.

As I navigate the school corridors, an eerie silence resonates. It is the tranquil aftermath of a storm, the hush blanketing a battlefield post-conflict. Inside, I feel like a truck has plowed into me. My emotions are a jumbled wreck, my heart fluttering like an injured bird. I feel painfully exposed, my deepest secrets laid bare for public scrutiny.

However, on the exterior, I maintain my composure, holding my head high. I set my gaze forward, focusing on the exit, the tantalising promise of freedom. Each step resonates in the silence, a testament to my resilience, a bold counter to the ordeal I've just survived. With every footfall, my resolve solidifies, my strength replenishes. It's akin to striding through a blaze, the intense heat both searing and purifying.

While I might be leaving the school physically, I am internally transitioning into a new chapter of my life. A chapter where I no longer have to shroud my true self. A chapter where I can display my identity with pride, not as a mark of shame.

Upon reaching the school gates and stepping into the open air, I draw a deep breath. It tastes of liberty, acceptance, self-love. It tastes of a life that's mine to live, mine to own.

Behind me, I abandon the mask, the facade, the fear of exposure. I leave behind the Ethan who shrinks away, who hides, who rejects his truth.

Ahead lies uncertainty, challenges and trials, and those who will persist in their mockery and hatred. But I'm prepared. I'm ready to confront them directly. I'm ready to battle. Because now, I'm not just fighting for myself. I'm fighting for every gay boy thrust into the light before readiness, every individual grappling to accept their truth.

As I distance myself from the school, I acknowledge that I'm moving away from the person I once was. In his stead, a new Ethan emerges. An Ethan who is unapologetically himself, strong, brave. An Ethan who is, finally, free.

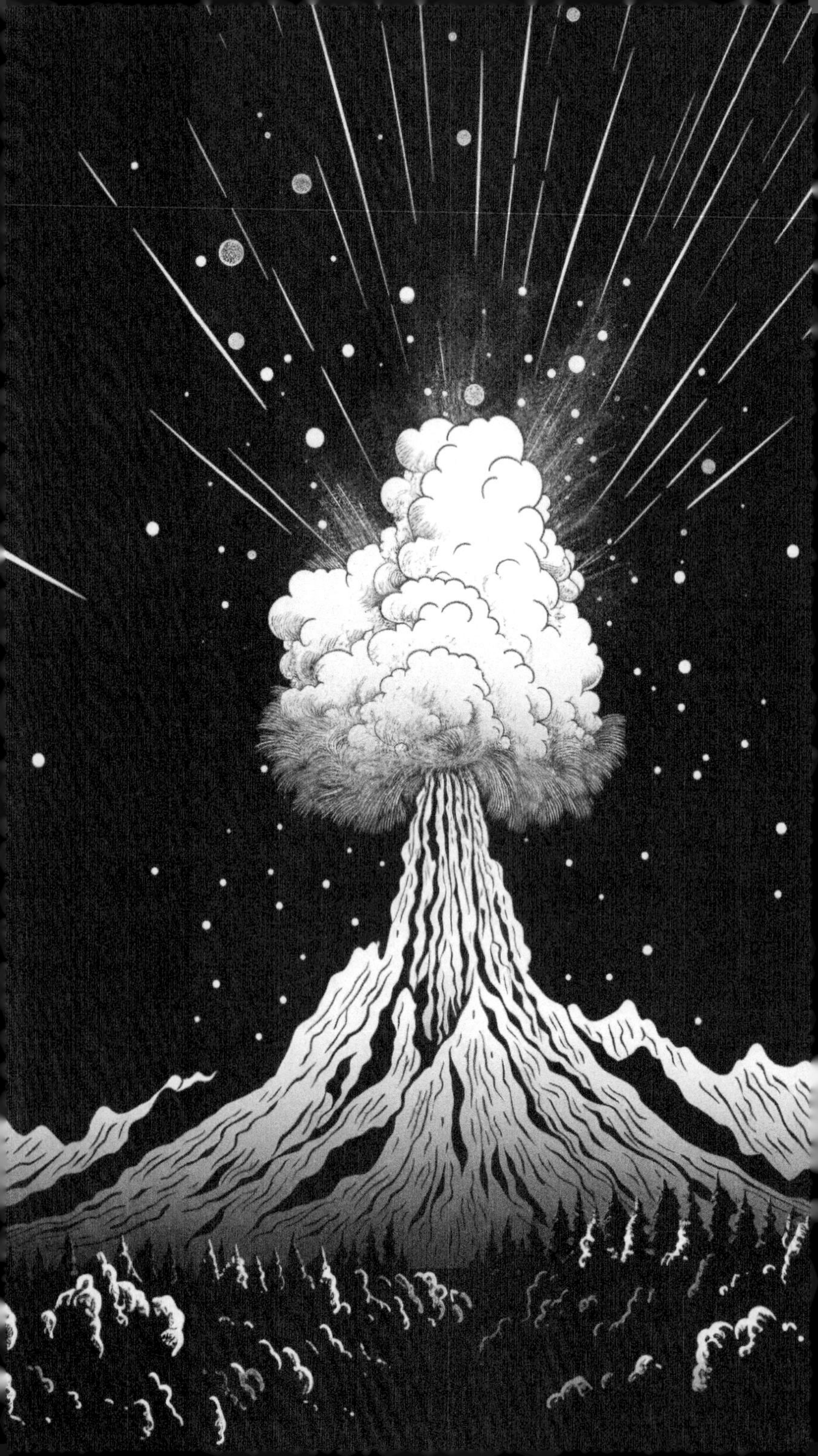

10

SEISMIC SHOCKS

I feel like a fugitive, pursued by my own thoughts, my own fears. Home, which once served as my refuge, is now a battlefield, the atmosphere heavy with unvoiced questions and confused concern. The whispers behind closed doors are almost audible, hushed dialogues in subdued tones, filled with worry and silent blame. Each unspoken word, each unasked question, serves as a burning reminder of the upheaval I'm experiencing. I feel trapped, besieged by their anxious glances, their inquisitive eyes seeking answers I'm not prepared to provide.

My heart thumps in my chest like a drum, each beat echoing the hurtful taunts hurled at me today. I need an escape—somewhere away from the interrogating stares, the stifling silence, the oppressive weight of my parents' worry permeating the air.

I seek refuge, a space where I can breathe, where I can consolidate my scattered thoughts, mend my shattered emotions. I yearn for a sanctuary where I can heal, where I can find peace. I need to be in a place where I can be myself, free from the perpetual fear of judgement, where I'm not compelled to don the facade society insists upon.

Unconsciously, my steps guide me to the one place that has provided solace during the bleakest periods of my life—the hospital. This cold, sterile environment, reeking of antiseptics and filled with soft undertones of muted conversations, offers peculiar comfort. The familiar corridor, the gentle hum of fluorescent lights, the tranquil demeanour of nurses and doctors—it all elicits a sense of solace.

The hospital has served as a unique haven for me. Here, among the white walls and beeping machines, I find comfort. This is where I met Alex, where our friendship flourished amid shared secrets and quiet companionship. This is where I discovered a part of myself unknown before, where I learned to accept my identity. Here, I feel secure, listened to, understood. It's my haven amidst the tumultuous seas of life, my guiding lighthouse through the fog of uncertainty.

As I traverse the corridor, a wave of determination engulfs me. Despite the inner chaos, I realise this is exactly where I need to be. This is where I can recover, where I can regain my strength. I am prepared to confront whatever awaits, ready to fight, to defend my ground. For that, I need Alex—I need the comforting presence of my friend, my confidante, my beacon in the storm.

The hospital's white corridors bring strange calm. Each step propels me further from the harshness of the outside world, deeper into the shell of this place which feels like a second home. I anticipate reaching Alex's room with a sense of eagerness, longing to see his radiant smile and hear his soothing voice. In his company, I feel acknowledged, not for my sexuality, but for who I am at my core—just Ethan, plain and simple.

However, as I push open the door to Alex's room, expecting to find his familiar figure propped up on the bed, a chill courses down my spine. The room is vacant—the bed immaculately made, the chair void of Alex's belongings, all wiped clean, devoid of any trace of his presence. A shiver of panic begins to infiltrate my veins, its icy tendrils encircling my heart.

Where is Alex?

In the sterile quietude of the empty room, the sudden sound of my phone dialling reverberates off the walls, each ring echoing Alex's absence mockingly. I press the phone firmly against my ear, my heartbeat synchronising with each resonating ring.

"Pick up, Alex," I whisper into the receiver, a desperate appeal into the void. But the silence on the other end swallows my words. There's no answer, not even the comforting hum of his voice on the voicemail. Just a void, an expanding chasm threatening to swallow me whole.

Anxiety grips me, and I detach from the call to start texting, the screen's blue light casting an uncanny glow on my face in the dim room.

> Are you okay?

> Where are you?

> Please reply :'(

The messages pour out, each more urgent than the last, only to be met by the biting silence of unanswered texts.

As the minutes morph into a torturous eternity, my mind spirals into chaos. It races down shadowy corridors, imagining horrific scenarios that chill my heart. Is Alex in pain? Is he alone somewhere, in need of help? Or could he be...

"No," I mutter, shaking my head as if to disperse the terrible thoughts. "Don't think like that, Ethan. He's okay."

Every question feels like a jolt of fear in my stomach,

exacerbating the sinking sensation that's taken hold of me. The lack of his voice, his laughter, his reassuring presence only amplifies my dread. Alex is my pillar, my lighthouse in the stormiest seas, and without him, I'm untethered, adrift amidst the turmoil of my fears and uncertainties.

Yet, through the panic, one fact crystallises even more: Alex is more than a friend, more than a companion or confidant. He's my lifeline, my anchor. His absence carves a gaping chasm, echoing with anxiety and a profound sense of loss. I need him now, more than I've ever needed anyone or anything before.

The weight of this realisation magnifies the room's silence, morphing it from a mere physical absence into a significant emotional void. Without Alex's steadfast presence, I'm truly alone. And that terrifies me more than anything else.

I force myself to breathe, attempting to temper the wild pounding of my heart. With renewed determination, I stride toward the reception desk, my eyes locked on the receptionist.

"Where's Alex?" I demand, my voice betraying a touch of desperation. The receptionist looks up, her gaze resting on my distressed countenance. She recognises me, she knows who I am.

"I'm sorry, I can't divulge any information..." she begins, but I interrupt her.

"He's my friend. I need to know he's okay," I implore, my heart pounding strong in my chest.

As my words linger, the receptionist hesitates, her gaze softening. But before she can answer, the silence is punctured by the sharp ring of her phone.

As she attends the call, I'm left standing, my heart drumming in my ears, anxiety tying knots in my stomach. I feel like I'm teetering on the edge of a cliff, precariously balanced between relief and panic, the uncertainty gnawing at me from the inside. Alex, where are you?

The hospital's air, once comforting, now feels dense with suspense. The white walls reflect my fears, and the sterile scent of disinfectant does nothing to soothe my racing heart. As the minutes trudge by, each unbearably slow, I grapple with my worry, my mind teeming with worst-case scenarios.

All I can do is wait, desperately hoping Alex is okay. Because I need him. Now more than ever. I need his smile, his calming presence, his understanding. Amidst my upheaval, I need the one person who makes me feel accepted as I am. And he's nowhere to be found.

The receptionist's gaze refocuses on me, her lips forming a thin line of professional restraint. "I'm sorry, but I cannot share any patient information unless you are a family member."

My heart thumps against my ribs, each beat a desperate entreaty. "Please," I plead, my voice barely louder than a whisper. "I need to know."

"Please," I insist once more, my voice weaving through the static silence enveloping the reception. "Please, you don't understand. He... he's my friend. My best friend."

For a moment, she remains quiet, her eyes mirroring my desperation. My heart drums like a wild creature caged within my chest, each beat echoing my plea.

"I just... I need to see him," I persist, my voice breaking on the tears I'm struggling to hold back. "I just need to know he's okay."

Her gaze softens, sympathy crossing her features. But her professional facade doesn't falter, her lips maintaining their firm line. "I understand your concern, but..."

I don't let her finish. "No, you don't understand!" I explode, words tumbling out in a frenzied rush. "You don't grasp his significance to me. How much... how much I need him."

My fingers grip the edge of her desk, knuckles blanching under the strain. "He's my everything," I admit, my voice dwindling to a whisper. "He's my lighthouse in the storm, my anchor. And I... I can't lose him. I can't."

She pauses, her fingers stilled above the keyboard. Her eyes meet mine again, now imbued with deep comprehension. "I'll see what I can do," she murmurs. And then she asks, "What's his full name?"

A glimmer of hope reignites, lending me the strength to reply. "Alex Devereux," I manage, each syllable a plea in itself.

As her fingers flutter over the keys, a desperate prayer forms in my heart, repeating Alex's name like a sacred chant. His image floods my mind, his laughter resonating in my ears, his smile lingering before my eyes. The receptionist's expression hardens, a look of dread washing over her features yanking me from my thoughts. I feel my heart plummet into a chasm. The words she utters next confirm my darkest fears.

"I'm sorry, Ethan... Alex... he passed away last night."

The remainder is a blur, a vortex of agony and despair threatening to devour me. As I stagger away, her words of consolation dissolve into the ambient noise. The world collapses around me. It feels as if a hole has been punched straight through my heart. Air whooshes out of my lungs, leaving me gasping. Alex... gone? It can't be.

Time seems to stand still, the hospital falling into an uncanny silence. I can hear the receptionist still speaking, her voice distant and muffled, as though emerging from underwater. But her words don't register. All I can focus on is Alex's smile, his laughter, the vibrant twinkle in his eyes. And now, he's...

My legs buckle, and I collapse to the floor, a shattered shell. Numbness envelops me, an overwhelming void consuming me. My vision blurs, the hospital's sterile white walls undulating before my eyes. It's as if I'm spiralling into a pitch-black abyss, the light extinguished from my world.

Alex was my lighthouse, my steadfast anchor in life's tempestuous sea. He saw beyond my sexuality, he saw the genuine me. And now, he's vanished. I feel like a vessel adrift at sea, violently tossed by the monstrous waves of despair.

Tears stream down my face, my body shuddering with sobs. The world seems to constrict, the vast cosmos imploding to a single point of agony and loss. The apocalypse has occurred, its devastation more catastrophic than I could ever envision. I remain alone in its aftermath, my heart fragmented into countless shards, my soul screaming for the one person who's no longer there.

My knees adhere to the frigid hospital linoleum, my entire body quivering as wave after wave of reality crashes over me. The floor beneath me feels as though it's shifting, the entire world tilting precariously. The fluorescent lights overhead glare remorselessly, their frosty illumination seeming a mockery of my despair.

Each second elongates into an eternity, a torment of silence punctuated only by the harsh, ragged rhythm of my breathing. The receptionist's voice echoes in my ears, a death knell that has obliterated my world. "Alex... he passed away last night."

Passed away. As if it's merely another mundane aspect of existence. But it's not. It's an earthquake, a hurricane, a cataclysm that's torn through my life, ripping everything asunder. I feel adrift in a sea of grief, bombarded by an onslaught of emotions I barely comprehend.

I thought I understood what it was to suffer, to feel lost and isolated. The public exposure had been a brutal assault, my sexuality thrust into the limelight in the harshest manner conceivable. It was a wound, profound and painful, that still pulsed raw and livid. But this... this is an entirely different realm of agony.

This is devastation of an unprecedented scale, a consuming black hole that absorbs all light, all joy, all hope. Alex's death isn't just an event, it's an apocalypse. It's the end of the world, the cessation of everything that had meaning to me.

Tears flow unchecked, a torrent reflecting the turmoil within my heart. They course down my face, drenching the front of my shirt, their salty taste acrid on my lips. I'm crying for Alex, for our forfeited future, for all the moments that will never exist.

Each sob that wracks my body is a mute scream, my heart vocalising its raw, agonising torment. I'm in mourning, grieving a loss so profound it threatens to shatter my very being. But beyond that, I'm drowning. Submerging in a sea of grief, assailed by relentless waves of pain that break over me, each more devastating than the last.

Succumbing to the despair feels like the only viable option. I let it engulf me, succumbing to its frigid, pitiless grasp. I yield to the pain, the sorrow, the crushing enormity of the void now occupying me. The boy I was, the boy who laughed, loved, and dreamed... he's disappeared. All that remains is a hollow husk, a lifeless phantom meandering through a world void of any significance.

The world as I knew it has ceased to exist. The laughter, the joy, the love... all erased in a heartbeat. The ground beneath me has crumbled, the sky collapsed, the stars extinguished. Amid the wreckage, in the ashes of my shattered existence, all that remains is the hollow shell of the boy I used to be. A boy lost in the aftermath of the apocalypse, his heart etched with the scars of a love extinguished too soon.

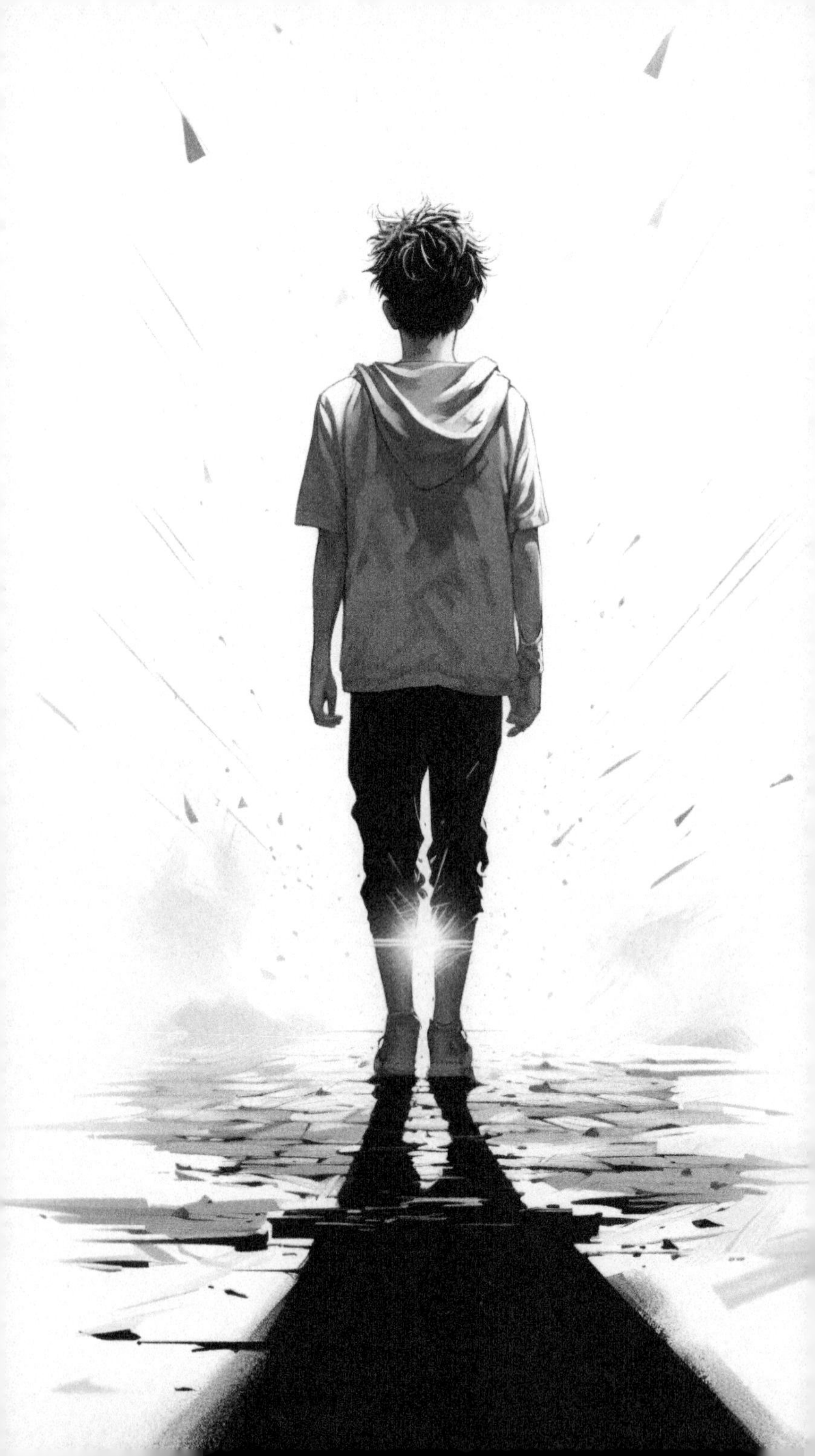

11
STEPPING INTO LIGHT

"Ethan," calls a voice that seems impossible yet familiar. It breaks through the fog of my grief, piercing the sorrow that encases me.

As I turn around, my heart beats a frantic tattoo in my chest. There, standing a few feet away from me, is Alex. He's alive, he's here, with wide, worried blue eyes, and his mouth calls my name repeatedly as if to convince me of his reality.

"Alex?" I whisper, my voice shaky. I blink several times, convinced I am hallucinating. Yet he remains, his image steadfast rather than a cruel figment of my imagination.

"Ethan, what's wrong? You look like you've seen a ghost," he says, rushing towards me. His hand reaches out to touch my shoulder. I flinch, expecting to feel nothing, but his touch is solid, warm, real.

"Where were you?" I croak, tears streaming down my face. "I called... I sent you messages... I thought..."

My words trail off, my breath hitching as I try to suppress the sobs threatening to escape. Alex looks at me, confusion etching lines onto his forehead. He moves his hand to cup my face, his thumb wiping away my tears.

"Hey, hey," he murmurs, his voice soothing. "I'm sorry, Ethan. My phone died and I was with my mom celebrating the good news."

"Good news?" I echo, my mind struggling to process the flood of information. The emotional whiplash from thinking he's gone to him being here, alive and well, feels overwhelming.

Alex's face breaks into a smile, the one that reaches his eyes and makes them sparkle. "Yeah, the good news that my sickness... it's finally leaving my body."

His words hang in the air, a beacon of light piercing the dark fog that envelops me. The weight crushing my chest lessens, the knot in my stomach untwisting. Alex is here. He's alive. He's recovering.

It feels like a dam breaks inside me, the relief overwhelming. A strangled sob escapes me, the tears returning but this time, they are of relief, of joy. I stumble forward, wrapping my arms around him in a fierce hug.

"You're okay," I murmur into his shoulder, the words more for myself than him. "You're okay."

He hugs me back just as tightly, his hand rubbing soothing circles on my back. "I'm okay, Ethan. I'm here."

For a long moment, I cling to Alex, his strong arms encircling me, lending me his strength. As I stand there, nestled against him, the surreal events of the day blend into an indistinguishable blur. The warmth radiating from Alex, the steady rhythm of his heartbeat against my body, the soft sound of his breath - they serve as my touchstones, my lifelines amidst the chaotic whirlpool of emotions.

His scent is comforting, the familiar blend of his cologne and the faintly clinical smell of the hospital, a constant reminder that he is real, that he is here. His hand, still rubbing soothing circles on my back, grounds me, pulling me back from the precipice of despair I teeter on just moments ago. He is alive. He is okay. He is here.

The fact that Alex is alive, well, and recovering feels like a miracle. The rush of relief washes over me in powerful waves, leaving me breathless and shaky. My tears have soaked through his shirt, but he doesn't pull away, doesn't release me. He holds me close, lending me his strength until I gather my own.

Gradually, my breathing syncs with his. My sobs subside, replaced by shaky sighs of relief. I raise my head to look at him, meeting his concerned blue gaze that is so full of life, so full of promise. Our eyes lock, communicating what words cannot, an intimate exchange that tightens our bond.

It's surreal, the contrast between the Ethan who walked into the school this morning and the Ethan who stands here now. I've faced my fears, been broken and put back together in the span of a few hours. It's an emotional crucible that I have emerged from, stronger and more resilient.

Alex is the sun in my world, illuminating my path, warming me from within. The chaos of the day has stripped us bare, torn away the facades we often hide behind. But in the end, it's him and me, standing strong amidst the rubble, our bond fortified by the trials we have faced.

In the end, I have not just found Alex, I have also found a piece of myself that I didn't know I was missing. It's the part of me that can stand up to bullies, the part that can survive being outed, the part that can face my worst fears and emerge on the other side, bruised but unbroken.

And as I stand there, holding Alex, his heart beating steadily against mine, I know. I know that no matter how chaotic, how painful, how heartbreaking the storm may be, as long as we are together, we can weather it. We can survive it. Because he is here, with me. He is okay. And in that moment, that is all that matters. That is all I need to know.

As we pull apart, Alex shoots me a reassuring smile. He extends his hand, beckoning someone from the sidelines. From the corner of my eye, I catch sight of a figure standing at a respectful distance.

"Come on," he says, tugging gently at my arm, "there's someone you should meet."

Alex then leads me towards his mother, the reassurance of his presence grounding me in this new yet overwhelming reality. As he introduces me to his mother, I finally feel a semblance of calm washing over me despite the whirlpool of emotions still swirling inside me.

"Mom," Alex says, turning towards the older woman with a bright smile. "I want you to meet Ethan, the person I can't stop talking about." His arm rests warmly around my shoulders as his mother extends her hand towards me.

"It's lovely to finally meet you, Ethan," she shares, her eyes sparkling with an inviting warmth. "Though I wish it weren't under such distressing circumstances. Alex has spoken so fondly of you, often."

A smile tugs at my lips, a small comfort in the tempestuous sea of my emotions. "The feeling is mutual, Mrs. Devereux."

Sharing a knowing glance with Alex, she gives a soft smile and nods. "I can see you two might appreciate some privacy. I'll come back later, if that's alright?" Her question is directed to Alex, who confirms with a gentle nod of his own. With a final tender look at us, she gracefully departs, her soft footsteps echoing in the otherwise silent corridor.

Alex then suggests we move to a more tranquil setting - a small park adjacent to the hospital. We amble outside, the stark, sterile atmosphere of the hospital gradually giving way to the vibrant, alive environment of the park. The contrast is jarring but soothing, the vibrant greens and blues a stark departure from the bleak hospital corridor.

The day is sunny, the warmth of the sun rays on my skin a soothing balm against the turmoil that had consumed the earlier hours. We find a quiet, secluded spot on the lush grass, the carpet of green a soft cushion beneath us. We sit side by side in a comforting silence, the only sounds the gentle rustle of leaves and distant laughter of children playing. The scent of freshly mowed grass, sweet and earthy, wafts through the air, grounding me in the reassuring mundanity of the moment.

Alex disrupts the silence, his voice soft, tentative. "So, what happened, Ethan?"

I blink. Swallow. I find myself fiddling with a strand of grass, unable to meet his eyes. "I... I thought you were... gone," I admit, my voice barely a whisper over the rustling leaves.

He stammers, his eyes, usually filled with vitality, wide with shock. "Gone? But why would you...?"

"The receptionist... she said Alex Devereux had... passed." The words spill out, leaving a bitter taste on my tongue.

His face crumples, lips parting, eyebrows furrowing in confusion. "But... that can't be..." he starts to protest, only to halt mid-sentence. Suddenly, realization dawns on him. "Wait. Did she say 'Alex Devereux' or 'Alexander Devereux'?"

Confusion churns within me. "She said 'Alex'... What difference does it make?" I ask, my heart pounding with a sudden rush of hope.

He sighs, lying back and staring at the open sky. "Ethan, my full name isn't just Alex Devereux. It's Alexander Pierre Devereux Pison. There's another Alexander Devereux in the hospital..."

Suddenly, everything clicks into place. I sit upright, staring at him, the gravity of his words sinking in. "You mean... it was another 'Alex Devereux' who...," I can't finish the sentence, the reality too overwhelming, too painful.

Nodding, Alex reaches for my hand, his grip warm and comforting. "I'm so sorry, Ethan," he whispers, his voice laced with regret. "The thought of you believing I was... I can't even imagine how you must have felt..."

"But you're here," I whisper back, the harsh reality too raw to voice any louder. "That's all that matters."

Looking at him, relief washes over me. A small smile creeps onto my face. "It's okay, Alex. You're here now, and that's what's most important." Our eyes meet, a silent promise passing between us - whatever challenges lie ahead, we'll face them together.

"But there's more," I confess, my gaze shifting from the vast sky to his azure eyes. His brows furrow, prompting me to press on.

"The truth is, I came to the hospital because I needed to see you, Alex," I admit, my voice trembling with emotion. "After what happened at school today... I just... I needed you."

A shadow weaves its way across his face, a reflection of worry casting deep pools in the vibrant blue of his eyes. "What happened there?" he inquires, his grip on my hand strengthening, the warmth reassuring.

The memories flood back, an unbidden torrent, a whirlwind of vivid recollections and raw emotions I'd been holding at bay - the humiliation, the rage, the dread. Yet amidst it all, an undeniable sense of relief of having finally stood up for myself.

Taking a deep breath, I begin to share my day with him. Each detail unfurls, from the moment I stepped into school flaunting my fresh look, the confrontation with the bullies, their heinous act of exposing my secret, and finally, the truth's crescendo when I stood tall, addressed the entire school, and accepted myself wholeheartedly.

As I narrate the series of events, Alex's face transitions

through a succession of emotions - shock gives way to outrage, and finally, a surge of pride replaces all else. Once I cease speaking, silence drapes us, a companion to the faint whisper of the grass rustling and the distant hum of the city's life pulsating.

When Alex breaks the silence, his voice resonates with a sincerity that sends a jolt through me. "Ethan," he initiates, the sound of my name from his lips now familiar and comforting. His eyes lock onto mine. "You're the bravest person I know."

I blink, taken aback by his proclamation. His words, humble and genuine, brimming with admiration, vibrate within me, aligning with the newfound power coursing through my veins, affirming my valour, my resolve, my defiance.

"Why...why would you say that?" I ask, my voice barely louder than a murmur. My heart hammers in my chest, each beat echoing his words.

He grins, a soft, warm smile that seems to light him up from the inside. "Because, Ethan," he begins, his hand reaching out to cradle my face tenderly, "Not many people have the courage to stand up to their bullies like you did. Not many people have the strength to face their fears, to reveal their true selves in front of an entire school."

His words linger, painting a vivid image of my day - the turmoil, the defiance, the acceptance. I close my eyes, permitting his words to penetrate my defences, to seep into the fissures of self-doubt, to mend the wounds I'd been nursing.

"And for that," he continues, his thumb gently tracing my cheek, "For your strength, your bravery, your defiance, Ethan, I am in awe of you. I am honoured to know you."

His words wrap around me, a warm embrace, leaving me breathless. My eyes flutter open, connecting with his sincere gaze. "I'm just relieved you're okay, Alex," I respond, my voice wavering with emotion. "That's all that truly matters to me."

A comforting silence descends, punctuated by unspoken words, and a shared understanding that transcends verbal communication. Our intimate world is momentarily disrupted by the rustle of leaves, a gentle breeze meandering through the park, carrying with it the fragrant scent of nearby blossoming flowers.

And then, the world contracts to the mere inches between us. Alex leans in, his gaze dropping to my lips. His hand, warm against my cheek, grounds me as he bridges the gap. His lips meet mine in a gentle, tender kiss, an unspoken affirmation of our mutual connection, our shared bravery.

As the shared sweetness of our kiss dissolves, I gently pull back, my gaze returning to meet Alex's. His eyes are a blend of relief and joy, a mirror to my own turbulent emotions. "So," I begin, my voice a soft murmur barely breaching the tranquility of the park, "you said your sickness is leaving your body?"

Alex nods, a radiant smile spreading across his face, pushing away the shadows of our shared fears. "Yes," he affirms, excitement bubbling under his calm exterior. "That's what my doctor told me this morning. My recent results are promising. Very promising. The treatment is proving effective, and if everything continues as is, I might reach remission soon."

His words, so hopeful and heavy with meaning, reverberate in the quiet air between us. My heart responds with a leap, a tidal wave of relief washing over me. This is the news we've been clinging to, praying for, every waking hour. Overwhelmed, I find myself bereft of words, unable to articulate the vast elation unfurling within me.

"But," he adds, his tone sobering, a stark contrast to the

jubilant news, "I still have a long journey ahead. There will be additional treatments, more examinations. It won't be easy, Ethan."

His words hang in the air between us, a sober reminder of the hurdles yet to be overcome. Relief, jubilation, hope—they all mingle within me, creating a whirlpool of emotions that threatens to topple my newfound equilibrium.

"That's incredible, Alex," I stutter, finally breaking free from my dumbfounded silence. "I don't even know what to say. This is the best news I've heard in—I can't even remember when."

Inhaling deeply, I tighten my grip on his hand, grounding myself in the tangible connection between us. "When you weren't in your room, when the receptionist told me—I feared the worst had happened," I confess, a shiver running down my spine at the haunting memory. "I thought I'd lost you."

Our eyes lock in a silent communion, reflecting not only the shared relief but also the vestiges of past fears, the remnants of nightmares that had so nearly become our reality. But amidst the turmoil, a glimmer of hope shines—a dim, flickering light that strengthens with each passing moment.

"And now, to hear this, to know that you're getting better, that you're going to be okay—it's beyond anything I could have hoped for," I choke out, my voice thick with emotion. "You're not just surviving, you're fighting. And you're winning."

Tears prick at my eyes, and a shaky laugh bubbles up from the pit of my stomach. "I've never felt more grateful for anything in my life. Not just that you're recovering, but that you're here, that you're alive, that we're here together."

His hand tightens around mine, offering a reassuring squeeze. "We're in this together, Ethan," he whispers, the corners of his mouth quirking upwards in a tentative smile. "And we're gonna get through this. Together."

Yes, we will.

As the echoes of Alex's inspiring words linger in my mind, I lean in, pressing my lips to his once more. It's a tender kiss, ripe with promise and warmth, saturated with hope. We part after a moment, breathless, yet wearing identical smiles.

"I should probably get going," I finally suggest, glancing towards the hospital. "I need to get home, reach my parents before dinner."

A flicker of understanding illuminates Alex's eyes. "You're going to tell them, aren't you?" he questions, his voice soft, laced with a quiet kind of respect.

I nod, steeling myself for the upcoming conversation. "I have to. Before they hear it from anyone else."

Alex tightens his grip on my hand, a silent offer of the support I desperately need. "You're brave, Ethan. Braver than anyone I know. And remember, no matter what happens, I'm here for you."

I express my gratitude in a whisper, barely audible over the pounding rhythm of my own heart. "Thank you, Alex. For everything. For being there, for being... you. And for being alive."

With these farewell words, I rise from the ground, a whirlwind of emotions swirling within me. The next challenge looms, casting a daunting shadow. Until now, coming out to my parents seemed as daunting as scaling Mount Everest. My heart beats in tandem with my anxiety, resonating with the fear and anticipation of the conversation that awaits.

Yet, amidst the tumult of my emotions, an unexpected calm envelops me. I feel ready. There's a renewed clarity in my eyes, a newfound determination in my stance. I feel akin to a soldier stepping onto the battlefield, primed to confront whatever lies ahead. This time, my truth is my shield and my honesty, my weapon.

The winds of change stir, heralding the dawn of a new chapter in my life.

I, Ethan, am on a quest for authenticity, ready to brave the looming storm. I understand now that hiding is no longer an option. I must live my truth, loud and proud. As I walk home under the long shadows of the setting sun, I cling to that thought, that conviction, bracing myself for the next hurdle.

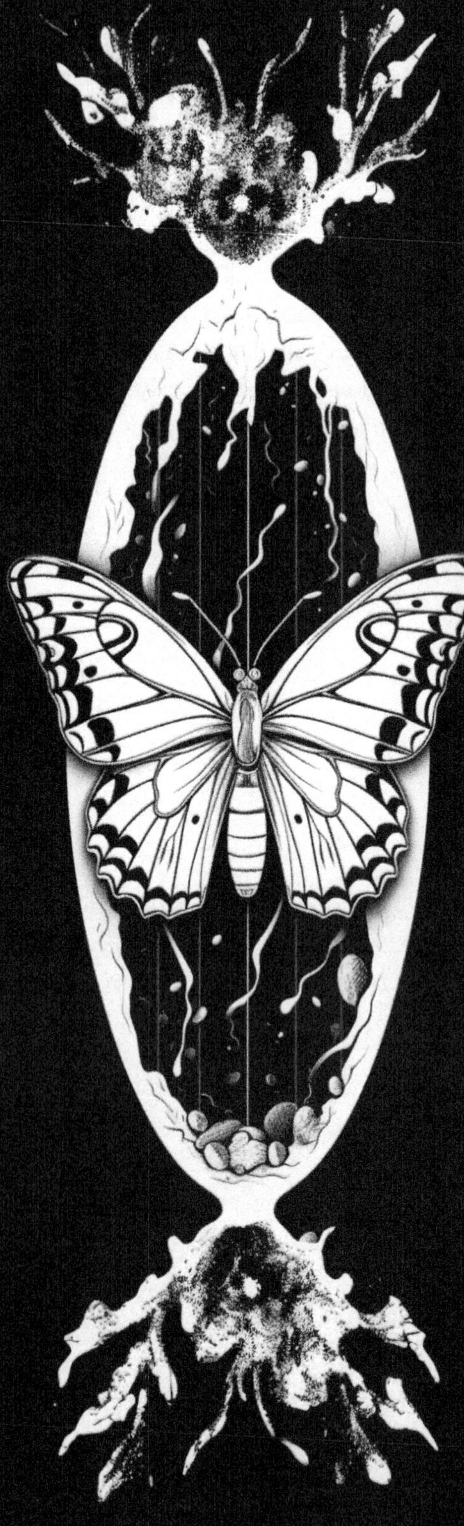

12
TRUTH UNVEILED

Standing at the threshold of our home, I am met by the inviting glow from the living room. Inside, my mother bustles around the dining area, positioning the last few utensils on the table. The comforting sounds of home – dishes clinking, the simmering pot on the stove, the muffled drone of the news from the adjacent room's television – stand in sharp contrast to the tempest brewing within me.

I draw a deep breath, allowing the familiar scent of home to envelop me, providing a fleeting solace before I immerse myself in the impending maelstrom. As I prepare to cross the threshold, a soft ping from my phone diverts my attention. A message from Alex.

> You've got this, Ethan.
>
> Good luck. <3

The simplicity of his words instills a warmth within me, rekindling my courage and momentarily pacifying my mounting anxiety. With a final glance at his message, I pocket my phone and step over the threshold. The door shuts with a soft click behind me, signalling the dawning of a new chapter in my life.

Dinner is a humble affair. The aroma of roasted chicken permeates the room, mingling with the scent of steamed vegetables and fresh rice. However, these enticing smells do little to divert my attention from the latent tension humming beneath the surface. The peaceful silence filling the room feels more akin to the tense calm that precedes a storm.

We convene at the table, bathed in the warm light of the chandelier overhead. To any outsider, this would appear as a perfect picture of a typical family dinner. Yet hidden under the veneer of tranquility, beneath the clatter of cutlery and my father's habitual recounting of his day at work, a storm is imminent, its dark clouds amassing in the pit of my stomach.

I aimlessly push the food around my plate, appetite eluding me. My gaze oscillates between my parents, my mind painting vivid pictures of potential reactions. Shock rippling across their faces as they struggle to understand? Disappointment creeping into their voices, replacing the familiar tones of affection? Anger igniting in their eyes, burning the bridge between us? Or could there be understanding, acceptance even, providing the shelter I crave?

My mind spins with a thousand questions, their intensity ratcheting up with each passing second. My heart thuds against my ribcage, like a trapped bird yearning for liberation. The words I need to utter loom large in the space around me, their weight growing heavier with each tick of the wall clock.

My hands shake slightly, causing the fork to rattle against the plate. I tighten my grip, attempting to steady myself, to summon the courage to articulate the words that have been stewing in my heart. Sweat beads on my forehead, and the knot in my stomach twists tighter with every second that ticks by.

I find myself on the precipice of a profound shift,

teetering between the familiarity of the life I've lived and the unknown that lies ahead. I stand on the cusp of my reality, ready to shatter the illusion I've been maintaining. I am on the verge of stepping into the eye of the storm, into the tumult. Despite the fear, despite the uncertainty, I am resolute in one thing – I need to speak up, to unveil the truth. For myself, for my parents, for my future.

My eyes oscillate between my parents, two pillars of stability in my turbulent world. Everything about them – their faces, expressions, habits – is familiar. Yet, in this instance, they feel curiously alien. I stand on the brink of disrupting our familial equilibrium, about to expose a facet of myself they never knew existed. The uncertainty looms, a spectre of doubt – will their warmth, their love, endure this revelation?

It feels as if the world contracts into the confines of our dining room, my heart's pounding rhythm reverberating in my ears, piercing the hushed silence. The room feels void of air, replaced by a tension so dense, it's almost tangible.

"Mom, Dad," I venture, my voice a mere whisper against the consuming quiet. "There's something I need to share with you. Something that's been within me for a long time."

Their gazes pivot towards me, a sea of curiosity replacing the familiar warmth in their eyes. A silence hangs in the air, heavy with anticipation and unspoken questions.

"I've been struggling, grappling with this truth about myself," I continue, the words tumbling out of my mouth, fragile and delicate. "It's something I've tried to understand, to accept. And now, I want you to understand and accept it too."

Taking a deep breath, I plunge into the confession that has been simmering within me for so long. "I'm gay," I finally admit, the words echoing in the ensuing silence, filling the void between us.

In the ensuing hush, the soft clinking of cutlery, the

rhythmic ticking of the wall clock - all recede into an uncanny quiet. My admission lingers in the air, a fragile sphere of truth in the midst of our picture-perfect family dinner.

With my heart pounding against my ribcage, its frantic rhythm amplified by the silence, I feel raw, exposed, akin to an open book awaiting judgment. At their mercy, I am suspended between acceptance and rejection.

My gaze hovers on their faces, seeking any hint of their feelings. Will they recoil, reject me? Or will they understand, accept me for who I am? The silence stretches, each ticking second a stark echo of the unveiled truth. Fear manifests as a chilling shiver coursing down my spine, its icy grip encasing my heart.

Yet amidst this fear, I taste an odd sense of liberation, a freedom that has been foreign for too long. I've unburdened my truth, casting off the shackles of pretence. Regardless of the outcome, I recognise that in this moment, I've made a significant stride towards authenticity, towards my true self.

My declaration reverberates through the room, a shockwave that echoes off the walls and settles into the quiet corners of our home. My father's fork freezes midway between his plate and his mouth, his attention riveted to my pale, earnest face. My mother's eyes remain fixed on her plate, her knuckles white against the fabric of the tablecloth. The room takes a collective inhale, as if bracing itself for what comes next.

"You're what?" My father's voice echoes through the silence, sharp and brittle. His eyebrows knit together, his eyes, usually warm and comforting, now hold a piercing gaze that bores into me.

"I'm gay, Dad," I reaffirm, pushing down the rising fear, forcing myself to maintain eye contact. The statement holds the weight of the world, a gravity that might either anchor or sink us.

My father's fork descends onto his plate with a clatter that slices through the oppressive silence. He rakes a hand through his hair, his expression a mosaic of disbelief and confusion, and another emotion I can't discern.

Across the table, my mother is silent, her figure rigid, her face unreadable. Always an open book with her emotions, her silence is unnerving, it blankets the room in a chill I hadn't anticipated.

"I know this can be hard to comprehend," I push forward, my voice barely above a whisper but resonating through the silence. "But I can't live under the weight of pretence anymore. This is me... the real me."

My words fill the room, hanging heavily in the air. They twist and writhe, etching a new reality into the comfortable fabric of our family life. My father's jaw clenches, his eyes swimming with unspoken questions. My mother finally lifts her gaze to meet mine, her eyes filled with a mixture of shock and something akin to comprehension.

"Pretending?" my father echoes, his voice choked with confusion. "You've been pretending all along?"

His words, devoid of anger, hit harder than I anticipate, but I don't falter. "Yes, Dad. Pretending to be someone I'm not. To fit into a world that wasn't designed for me."

He blinks at my words, his forehead furrowed as he grapples with my revelation. After what feels like an eternity, he releases a weary sigh, his tension noticeably ebbing. "Ethan," he starts, his voice steady. "I can't pretend I fully understand. But I know this - you're my son. Nothing changes that."

His words echo in the room, striking a chord within me. The love in his gaze douses the inferno of my fears. While his acceptance is a process, not an immediate shift, his response isn't a rejection. It's an unspoken promise, a commitment to try to understand, to journey into this unfamiliar territory together.

My father's unexpected words echo in my mind, sending waves of relief crashing through me. His response, far from the reactions I had braced myself for, strikes an offbeat chord of disbelief.

In our family, my father has always been an anchor, a rock of traditional values, painting our world in monochrome. Yet, now, he's stepping into uncharted territories, embracing an unfamiliar spectrum of hues – all for his son.

There will be storms of probing questions, the high tides of challenging dialogues, and periods of unsettling quiet. Yet beneath it all, an undercurrent of unconditional love remains.

I feel lighter, like Atlas himself has surrendered his world from my shoulders. My father's words ignite a spark of hope, hinting at a future brighter than the gloom-filled days I had been anticipating.

"I understand, Dad," I murmur, my voice hushed but determined. "We can figure this out together."

On cue, my mother's voice, soft yet firm, cuts through the poignant silence. "Ethan, is this why you've acting so different lately? I thought it was the hospital incident that changed you."

Her eyes are an emotional whirlpool – confusion, understanding, and most prominently, concern. Classic Mom, always aware, always caring. She had noticed the changes, the subtle shifts beneath my facade, and instead of forcing a confrontation, she'd given me room to navigate.

A wry smile tugs at my lips as I nod in agreement. "Yes, Mom, in a way, it is all interconnected."

She digests this, her gaze never straying from mine. Then, her hand reaches across the table, covering mine in a silent show of solidarity. "We'll get through this, Ethan," she assures me, her voice warm and sincere. "We always do."

Her words, brimming with such unyielding faith, fan the flames of hope within me. Hope for better days, hope for a new chapter in our lives, one where understanding and acceptance hold the pen.

As I look between my parents, gratitude wells up within me. They have chosen love, chosen family. And in this moment, that's more than enough.

The night is thick with raw, potent emotions. But as I retire to my room, a weight lifts from my chest. I've taken the needed actions towards living my truth. And as daunting as it is, it's equally liberating. For the first time, I am truly, a hundred percent myself.

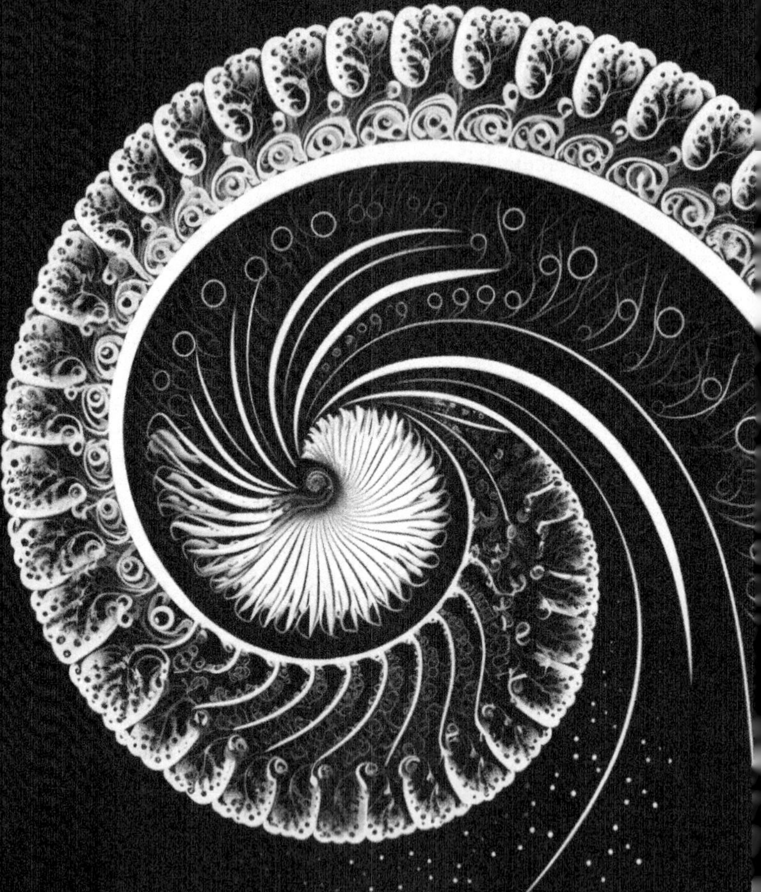

13
ECHOES OF CHANGE

The soft hum of my phone stirs me from sleep. As my eyes adjust to the glaring screen's brightness, a cascade of notifications rolls in, setting my heart to a rapid beat.

Social media, once a low hum in my life's backdrop, has exploded into a deafening chorus overnight. Over a hundred thousand followers on various platforms have joined my journey—a journey that only yesterday, I embarked on in solitude. Suddenly, it stands starkly public, far more public than I ever imagined.

A surge of disbelief washes over me with each notification. The sheer volume of the numbers is staggering. Clips of my impromptu school speech have spread far and wide, crossing borders, transcending continents. My face, my voice, my words echo back to me from countless posts, tweets, and comments.

The raw emotion and candid honesty that compelled me to speak up, to assert my identity in the face of blatant bigotry, have resonated with people worldwide. Comments pour in from different countries, different time zones, narrating the impact of my words. It's surreal. My journey, once personal and solitary, has been thrust into the public eye, inadvertently becoming a beacon of resilience and strength for others navigating similar paths.

Posts tagged with my name - praising my courage, sharing my story, echoing my words - flood my feed. There are reposts with extensive captions discussing my bravery, fan edits highlighting my speech, reaction videos commending my stance. My small world has exploded onto a global stage where I have become the unintentional lead act.

As I grapple with the enormity of what has transpired, my heart thuds in my chest. One moment of bravery, one declaration of my truth, has sparked a ripple effect beyond my wildest imagination. This wave transcends me. It's about all of us - silenced, marginalised, shamed for our differences. It's about our collective resolve, our united stand against bigotry.

A weight of responsibility, expectation, and hope settles on my shoulders. Yet, coupled with it, there's an exhilarating surge of liberation. My words, my truth, my identity have been seen, heard, recognised, and accepted by an unimaginable multitude. The journey that began in solitude is no longer just mine. It's shared, connecting and empowering countless individuals worldwide. Despite its intimidating nature, this realisation imbues me with a buoyant sense of hope and anticipation for the road ahead.

A deluge of supportive messages pours in from people of all walks of life - fellow students expressing admiration, LGBTQ+ individuals sharing their struggles, parents commending my bravery, educators advocating for inclusivity. This wave of solidarity warms my heart, offering solace against the storm my life has become. Words of encouragement and love from total strangers merge into a chorus of acceptance and empathy, causing my heart to swell with gratitude.

However, the symphony of positivity isn't devoid of dissonant notes. Every few messages are a stark reminder that not all embrace my unveiled reality. Derogatory slurs, threats, vitriolic diatribes perforate my inbox, the hateful intent oozing from the screen. The rebukes range from disgusted to threatening, their revulsion potent, condemnation clear.

Some implore me to recant, insisting it's a sick joke or a rebellion. Others question my integrity, my sanity. The ignorance is palpable, the bigotry glaring. Even those who used my truth as ammunition for ridicule in school have found their way here, their venom cloaked in righteous indignation.

Amid the sting of these hateful messages, a realisation plants itself. This polarity mirrors society's conflicted relationship with our existence. Our fight for acceptance battles not only outright hostility but also ignorance, intolerance, and indifference. The truth I've proclaimed, mirrored by countless others, rides the rollercoaster of public opinion. It's a reality we must navigate together, a battle we must engage with courage, education, and relentless perseverance.

Fear slithers around my thoughts, threatening to strangle my nascent excitement. The fear isn't solely about the backlash, potential alienation, judgment from peers, or loss of anonymity. It's the fear of raw vulnerability that comes with being pushed into the limelight, innermost truths laid bare for the world to see.

Yet, beneath the fear, a thrill bubbles. It's exhilarating, making my heart race, electrifying my skin. For the first time, I'm recognised for who I truly am. No hiding, no pretending. My voice rings out, crossing boundaries I never imagined breaching.

Every like, every share, every comment generates ripples. I'm reaching people who may be grappling with their truths like I did. I stand as evidence that it's okay to be true to oneself, to be different, to shatter societal norms and expectations.

I'm no longer just Ethan, the high school student navigating adolescence. I'm Ethan, the teenager who stood against bigotry, transforming a moment of ridicule into empowerment. I've become an unexpected beacon, a lighthouse in stormy seas for those lost, seeking, needing hope and courage.

The truth once used as a weapon against me has become my armour. It strengthens me, readies me for the looming storm. With each passing moment, I recognise the power within my truth, within my authenticity. It's not a power granted to me, but one that's been dormant within me, now awakened and ready to shine.

As my phone vibrates with a call, Alex's name on the screen startles me. He's been part of this journey, present at the genesis of my truth. He's more than a bystander; he's a thread woven into the fabric of my story.

Answering the call, I'm flooded with gratitude. I'm not alone. Despite the tumult and the uncertainty of what's to come, I have a confidant, a partner, an ally. With that thought, I steel myself to face the reverberations of change my truth has ignited.

The moment I connect the call, Alex's voice floods my ears, teeming with excitement. "Ethan!" he exclaims, every word infused with infectious energy. "What the hell is going on? I can't browse the internet without seeing your face."

His words coax a laugh from me, part amusement, part disbelief. "Tell me about it," I reply, sleep still clinging to my voice. "I woke to a social media tempest. I never expected the whole thing to explode like this."

"I mean, your speech was incendiary. It was... it was raw, brave, and unbelievably inspirational," Alex's voice softens, awe coating his tone. "It struck a chord with people, Ethan.

You stood up for yourself in a way many only fantasise about."

The memory of that day surges back to me – the fear, the pain, the defiance. How I seized control of the narrative, declaring my truth to an audience primed for my humiliation. My words, now rippling across the internet, impacting the lives of distant strangers, stand testament to that moment of undaunted courage.

"I was terrified, Alex," I confess, my voice barely more than a whisper. "I still am."

A brief silence ensues before Alex responds. "You know, it's okay to be scared. It's okay to not know what's next. What matters is you didn't let your fear prevent you from being yourself, from standing up for yourself."

His words tighten my throat. His voice carries no judgement, only understanding and pride. That pride kindles warmth in me, pushing back my fear and fostering fresh strength.

"I'm so proud of you," he affirms, sincerity in his voice stirring something deep within me. "Proud to know you, proud to have you in my life, and to be part of your journey."

His words linger in the silence that follows, their gravity more profound than I'd ever envisaged. I'm not alone in this. I have Alex beside me, his steadfast support a beacon guiding me through the storm.

"Thank you," I murmur, emotion constricting my words to a whisper. "Thank you for standing by me."

※

The morning sun has already staked its claim high in the sky by the time I glance at my watch. The unforgiving digits blink back at me, a stern rebuke of my tardiness. Cursing, I scramble to get ready, the echo of Alex's parting words of encouragement propelling me as I dash out of the house.

The school looms large and imposing as I approach the entrance, my heart drumming a nervous tattoo in my chest. I don't know what to expect. My words have echoed in the ears of thousands, perhaps even millions, by now. Will things be different? Will I be different?

Crossing the threshold of the school gates, I'm greeted by the familiar noise of chatter and laughter, the vibrant pulse of teenage life beating strong. Yet amidst this familiar scene, I notice a significant shift. The bullies, once parading through the hallways with an ill-conceived sense of superiority, are conspicuously absent.

There's a raw satisfaction in witnessing this reversal, the hunter becoming the hunted. The knowledge that my voice, my story, has engineered this change fills me with an unexpected swell of pride. I have confronted my fears, defended myself, and emerged victorious.

Throughout the day, I'm met with curious glances, hushed whispers, and even scattered words of admiration. The atmosphere is a stark contrast to the norm, a palpable shift in the air that only underscores the impact my words have had.

But amidst this whirlwind of change, one constant remains - Alex. His unwavering support, his shared exhilaration over the sweeping changes around us, serves as a comforting anchor in the tumultuous sea of transformation.

Walking down the hallways, with echoes of my speech still ringing in my classmates' minds, I sense a fresh awareness of myself. I've not only weathered the storm but have emerged from it stronger, more resilient, and without shame.

And it's not just me. The entire school appears to have undergone a metamorphosis, its outdated ways challenged by the raw, undeniable truth of my words. I see it in the students' interactions, in the way teachers address us, in the heightened sense of awareness and respect that permeates our shared spaces.

I've ignited a ripple, and it has expanded into a wave. A wave of change promising brighter days, gentler words, and a haven where everyone can comfortably be themselves. It's overwhelming and exciting, infusing me with a sense of hope that has been absent for far too long.

As the final bell tolls, signalling the end of another whirlwind day, I find myself lingering at my locker, a smile playing at the corners of my lips. The school is changing, I am changing, and it makes me feel... good.

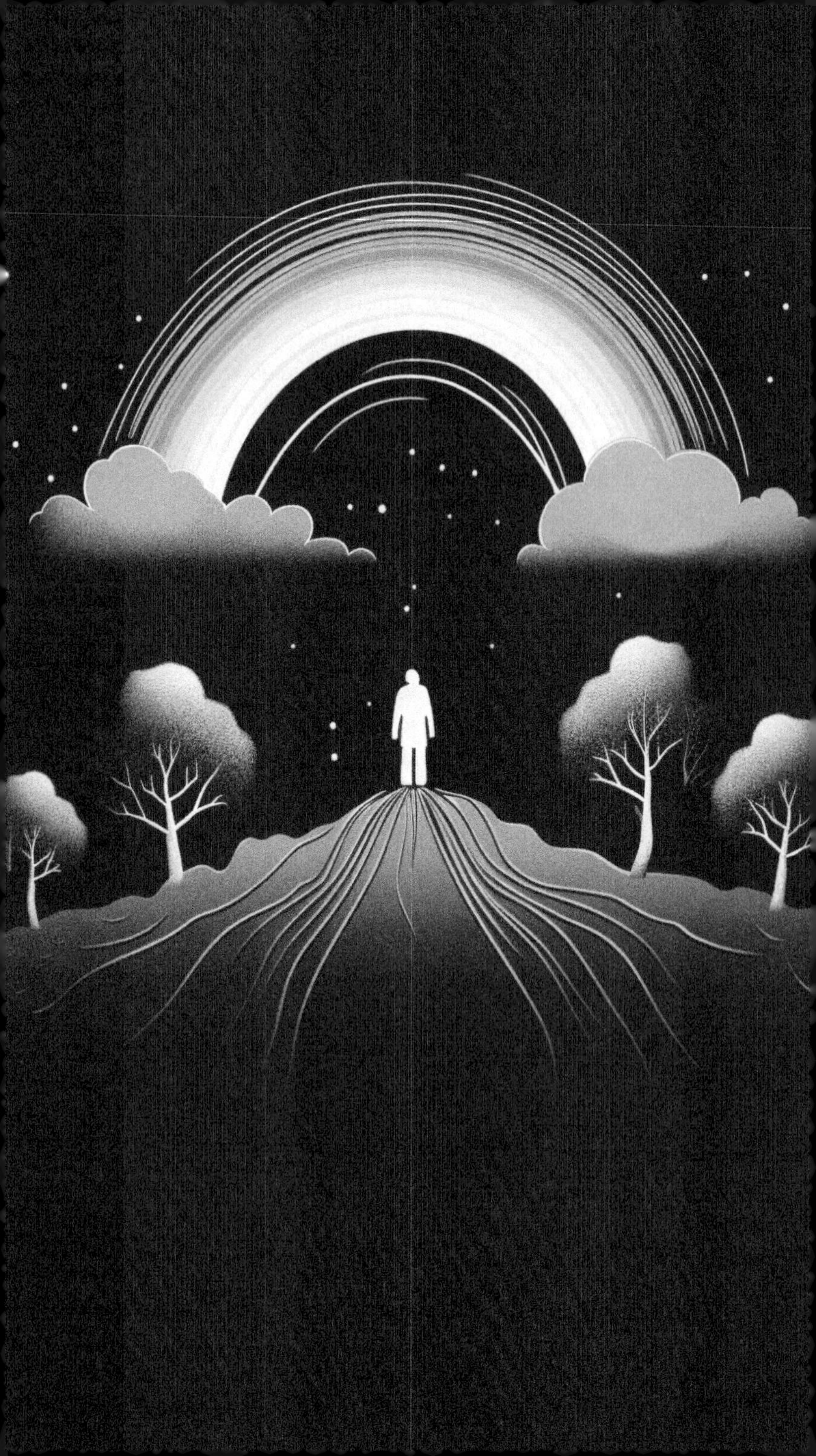

14
RISE ABOVE

Studio lights dance upon my face, igniting a tremor of anticipation within me. It isn't fear quickening my heart, but a profound sense of exhilaration. The stark white brightness casts a revealing light on every facet of my being, placing me squarely in the limelight. Each beam functions as a spotlight, illuminating not just me but every individual ever relegated to the shadows.

Across from me, the seasoned host sits. Sharp, intelligent eyes study me, emanating a blend of warmth and curiosity. Having presided over countless stories, witnessing an array of human experiences, she nevertheless leans forward, hands clasped, as a palpable shift permeates the atmosphere. The audience also leans in, their collective breath hushed in anticipation of our unfolding dialogue.

This isn't merely an interview; it's a testament, a reckoning. A moment that transcends the casual chit-chat characteristic of morning shows to navigate a realm that demands acknowledgment. The audience isn't merely observing a young man share his story; they're witnessing a narrative of love, acceptance, and defiance against oppression.

The silence enveloping us isn't borne of discomfort; instead, it's steeped in profound understanding. A tacit agreement that this conversation isn't only different, it's necessary. I'm not merely Ethan, the boy bullied and outed at school. I stand as a symbol, a beacon for every individual silenced, every voice trembling under the spectre of rejection and ridicule.

The weight of this moment is palpable, yet it doesn't bear me down. It uplifts me, filling me with a strength I hadn't known I possessed. Each blinding ray of light underscores that I am no longer hidden, no longer ashamed. I stand tall in my truth, lit by the brilliance of my existence.

In the sea of familiar and unknown faces in the audience, Alex's serves as my anchor. His eyes, resonating with deep understanding, bolster my courage to stand on this public platform and share my story. His hand has held mine through private moments of despair and triumph, his words have been my solace in self-doubt, and his unwavering belief has transformed my fear into bravery.

Beside him sit my parents, their expressions a mosaic of emotions. They've been my bulwark on this journey, their love turning into my strength. My mother's eyes well with tears, yet her lips curl in a proud smile. Her hand tightly clasped in my father's, who sits with silent, composed dignity. His silent nod of encouragement speaks louder than any words could.

The host offers a soft smile as she takes me in, her gaze reflecting the profound gravity of the moment. As she takes a breath to speak, the silence of anticipation yields to a wave of profound dialogue. A dialogue set to echo the sentiments of thousands of untold stories. A dialogue that will resonate with the beats of a thousand silenced hearts. And at the heart of that echo, I am ready to share my story.

"Good morning, everyone," the host's voice reverberates

through the studio, her enthusiastic tone rippling out towards the cameras focused on us. "Today, I am privileged to share the stage with a young man who has morphed into an overnight sensation, a symbol for our youth, a beacon of courage and honesty. He took a stand against homophobia, publicly embraced his truth, and has since inspired millions across the nation and beyond. Please join me in welcoming Ethan."

Her words cascade over me as I drink in the surreal reality of the moment, my heart pulsing with a cocktail of nervousness and exhilaration. Applause erupts from the audience, a sea of faces orienting towards me with anticipation, respect, and in some instances, hope. I inhale deeply, drawing fortitude from their collective enthusiasm, preparing to share my story on a scale far grander than I ever anticipated.

"Ethan," she commences, her voice a soft symphony of strength. "Your speech at your school became a beacon for so many people. Young individuals grappling with their identities are now looking to you for guidance. What do you wish to say to them?"

I inhale deeply, my heart reverberating in my chest. "Firstly, I want to say that you are not alone. I am all too familiar with the loneliness that can envelop you when you're wrestling with your identity. When you feel like an outsider, when the world around you appears uncomprehending. But always remember, there's an entire community out there who understands, who cares, and who will stand beside you."

My gaze flickers to Alex, evoking memories of the countless nights we spent talking, understanding, and bolstering each other. "I want you to know that it's okay to be scared, It's okay to be uncertain. It's okay to question. And it is more than okay to be different."

Tears gather in my eyes, a lump taking residence in my throat as I press on, "I want to assure you that it's okay to love whoever your heart chooses. Your love isn't lesser. Your feelings aren't invalid. You are not insignificant."

I swallow hard, a surge of purpose swelling within me. "You are beautiful, exactly as you are. Your identity is yours to explore, to comprehend, and to embrace. No one else has the right to delineate it for you, to pass judgment, or to make you feel any lesser due to it."

A pause envelops the room as I regain composure, my words settling into the hearts of everyone present. The host remains silent, her eyes brimming with unshed tears. Then she voices out, her tone barely above a whisper. "What about those who are gripped by fear, Ethan? Those who dread the judgment, the mockery?"

For a moment, I fall silent, her question's gravity weighing on me. Then, a smile blooms on my face, tinged with sadness but dominated by determination. "Fear is part of the process. It's a testament to the enormity of what you're experiencing. But don't allow the fear to hold sway. Don't let it discourage you from living your truth."

I gaze straight into the camera, my voice steady. "The world can be a harsh place. Yet, it can also be beautiful. It can accept, it can support. And the onus falls on us to sculpt that world. A world where love escapes judgment, where identities dodge ridicule, where every individual basks in the celebration of their unique self."

"Thank you, Ethan," the host interjects, clearing her throat to continue. "You've confronted challenges and exhibited immense courage. What supplied your strength?"

"I mined my strength from honesty," I commence, my mind reeling back to the day I was cornered into confronting my identity in front of the entire school. "Honesty directed at myself and the world. Recognising and embracing who I am. My strength was further bolstered by the support I received, from Alex, from my parents, and from those who stood by my side, believed in me."

A tear strays down her cheek as she nods. "And what about those who encounter resistance from their own families, their own friends? What message do you impart to them?"

"That's a challenging situation to navigate," I concede, my heart heavy with empathy. "What I can say is that sometimes, people need time to understand, to adjust. Be patient. And sometimes, you need to locate your chosen family. Those who understand you, support you, love you for your true self. There's an entire community out there ready to welcome you, to fight for you. You're not alone."

"And what about the bullies? The ones who try to oppress, who try to impose their narrow-minded views onto others?" Her voice takes on a steely quality, mirroring the resolve in my heart.

"To them, I deliver this message," I declare, my gaze unwavering, "Your bullying, your ridicule, your hatred, it emanates from a place of ignorance, from a lack of understanding. I hope that one day you educate yourself, you open your mind and your heart. Love is vast, diverse, beautiful. Don't confine it with your prejudice."

Moved by my words, the host chuckles. "And finally, Ethan, what does the future hold for you? On a personal level, perhaps?"

A smirk twitches at the corners of my mouth as I contemplate my future, my gaze meandering towards Alex in the audience. "Well," I start, a twinkle of mischief in my eyes. "Personally, I'm looking forward to lots of awkward date nights with Alex, numerous debates over which TV show will succumb to our next binge-watching session, and probably a surfeit of charred meals because neither of us harbours any culinary skills."

The audience explodes with laughter, and even the host chortles at my response. Alex is shaking his head at me, a blush creeping up his neck, but his eyes are warm, radiating love.

"But to address the matter seriously," I resume once the laughter has ebbed. "I'll persist in living my truth, inspiring others to mirror the same. I will remain an advocate for acceptance, for love, for understanding. I'll extend my support to those who need it and fight against those who propagate hatred."

As the echoes of our conversation begin to fade, the studio once again fills with applause. This time, however, it resonates in a way that extends beyond the confines of the studio. This thunderous applause isn't just a tribute to me; it's a grand symphony of support for anyone who has ever felt different, anyone who has ever endured the sting of concealing their truth. It's for every young person and adult within our rainbow community who are still living life in their glass closets.

Each clap, each cheer, symbolises solidarity with those grappling with their identities, those fearing the world's judgment. It's an anthem for the outcasts, for the 'others', for the brave souls daring to exist authentically in a world that too often feigns blindness. It's an affirmation of our shared struggles, our shared resilience, our shared victories.

As the lights dim in this poignant moment, a profound sense of peace settles within me. The journey is far from over; in truth, it's just beginning. An uncertain yet promising path sprawls ahead, radiant with the promise of acceptance, understanding, love. This path, fraught with challenges, is also laden with infinite possibilities.

Bathed in the twilight of a moment signifying both an end and a beginning, I stand on the precipice, awash with an unshakeable determination. I've weathered the storm, faced the spectre of judgment and emerged stronger. More than ever, I'm primed to stride towards a future where love isn't a source of shame, but a badge of honour, a testament to our shared humanity.

I gaze into the dimming lights, applause still reverberating in my ears, a triumphant symphony carrying the hopes and dreams of countless souls. The sounds transform into a vow, a pledge to myself and to every individual who's ever tasted the bitterness of being different.

We won't buckle under ignorance's weight or cower in bigotry's shadow. We won't embrace defeat or allow ourselves to be belittled, devalued. We'll rise, stand tall, and continue to soar, unshackled by fear or shame, until the world acknowledges us for who we truly are.

We aren't merely characters populating the margins of a mainstream narrative. We aren't footnotes in someone else's tale. We are the protagonists of our own lives, deserving of the spotlight, deserving of respect, acceptance. We are diverse, we are vibrant, we are real.

We come in different shapes, colours, sizes. We carry different stories, confront different struggles, harbour different dreams. Yet, we share a common truth. A truth that defines us, unites us, empowers us. Our love might differ, but that's okay. Because love, in all its forms, in all its hues, is valid. It's beautiful. It's human.

Thus, we will rise and continue to rise, persisting and shining ever brighter with each day. We'll drench the world in our colours and our love, allowing it to seep into every crevice. We will break down barriers, shatter prejudices, and enlighten hearts.

For we are not mere echoes in the void. We are a powerful chorus, a symphony of authenticity, ready to crescendo until our melody drowns out intolerance's clamour. We are here. We are proud. And we won't cease until the world hears our song, recognises our truth, celebrates our existence.

I am ready for whatever lies ahead. Ready to fight, to love, to live... unapologetically. For being true to who we are, standing tall in our truth, is the most triumphant victory of all.

And love always wins.

ACKNOWLEDGMENTS

I want to start by acknowledging two pillars of strength in my life: my sister Lara and my cousin Mai. Their unwavering support has been my constant, my compass in the stormy seas of life. They are the light that pierces the darkness, the fortress against life's hurricanes, my sanctuary amidst chaos. I extend my deepest gratitude to them for empowering me to embrace my true self, to dream fearlessly, and to chase those dreams relentlessly.

As I write this, I can't resist extending a quirky tip of the hat to an intriguing character in this current moment of my life, fondly code-named 'M.' M, your boundless energy and zest have added a distinct flavour to my current existence, like a surprise jalapeño in a mild pasta. Your presence in the recent months has been an exhilarating ride, providing unexpected fuel to the creative fire of this book. Exploring the multifaceted world of the rainbow with you has been a joy, even with the dissonant stars and all.

Lastly, to you, my cherished reader. You've gifted me your time, delved into my very first book, and for that, I am profoundly grateful. By stepping into this narrative, you've joined me on a journey both intimate and expansive. My hope is that this story resonates with you, that it touches your heart, challenges your assumptions, and maybe, just maybe, leaves you a little transformed. Thank you for embracing this adventure with me.

ABOUT THE AUTHOR

Iam Obsydian is a new voice in literature with a passion for shining a light on the LGBTQ+ experience. Drawing on personal journeys and a vibrant imagination, Obsydian infuses heartfelt authenticity into every story. Committed to increasing visibility and fostering understanding through writing, Obsydian's debut novel is just the first step in a promising literary journey. Stay tuned for the tapestry of tales yet to unfold.

instagram.com/IamObsydian
goodreads.com/IamObsydian